WISH

A
RECIPE
FOR
ADVENTURE

Copyright © 2023 Disney Enterprises, Inc. All rights reserved.
Design by Winnie Ho
Composition and layout by Susan Gerber

Published by Disney Press, an imprint of Buena Vista Books, Inc. No part of this book may be reproduced or transmitted in any form or by any means, electronic or mechanical, including photocopying, recording, or by any information storage and retrieval system, without written permission from the publisher. For information address Disney Press, 1200 Grand Central Avenue, Glendale, California 91201.

First Paperback Edition, November 2023
1 3 5 7 9 10 8 6 4 2
FAC-004510-23257

Printed in the United States of America
This book is set in Weiss.

Library of Congress Control Number: 2023938061
ISBN 978-1-368-09364-4

Visit disneybooks.com

SUSTAINABLE FORESTRY INITIATIVE
Certified Sourcing
www.forests.org
SFI-01681

Logo Applies to Text Stock Only

DISNEY
WISH

A
RECIPE
FOR
ADVENTURE

BY WENDY WAN-LONG SHANG

DISNEY PRESS
Los Angeles • New York

PROLOGUE

It is generally agreed the world over that the kingdom of Rosas is unrivaled in its beauty.

Rising elegantly above gentle aqua waves, the island is adorned with many rows of houses curling toward the great castle at its center and nestled among mountains, an orange grove, and a forested hamlet with lofty trees, green grass, and flowers.

The buildings are made of pale stone, and they stand side by side, snugly as dear friends, topped by blue-green roofs and linked by graceful arches, paved streets, and sweeping stairways. Cobblestone pathways meander through plazas—shaded with blossoming vines and attended by a bubbling fountain and a tranquil reflecting pool—and spill into the marketplace, framed with stalls of every assortment.

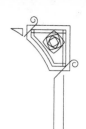

Each morning, the sun rises with pink, gold, and purple light stretching across the sky, and all day long, white-masted ships sail in and out of the harbor, bringing spices, bolts of cloth, letters, and tea.

The main import, though, is the throngs of people from far and wide, who visit Rosas with wide eyes and mouths hanging open. *How can such a beautiful place be possible, where everyone is content and welcomed and cared for?*

The highest point in Rosas is the castle of King Magnifico. It is said that the castle is the second most striking creation in Rosas, the first being, of course, the sorcerer-king himself, who can grant the deepest wishes of his people. That is why so many travelers come to see this place with their own eyes—to catch a glimpse of the magical king who regularly makes dreams come true.

Round tiers flow up the castle toward a single tower, which is enclosed by tall sparkling windows so that the king may watch over his subjects with care. The very top of the tower comes to a point, wrapped in the same blue-green tile as the rest of the buildings in Rosas. The townsfolk say it is a sign of how much their king loves them, to have a castle that looks like the father of all the buildings they live in.

There are rumors of what might be in that very top room of the castle. Some imagine that it is a sun-filled greenhouse growing flowers to further beautify Rosas; others say that it is a library teeming with leather-bound books and cushioned velvet chairs so that their benevolent king may read and grow wiser by the day.

However, in this beautiful kingdom, in this splendid, soaring structure, at least one person is certain that the most wonderful room in the whole of Rosas is not at the top of the castle at all, but at its very center, deep inside.

That person is Dahlia, the king's baker, and the space she holds so dear is the castle kitchens, of course.

Dahlia might, at first, remind an onlooker of a cardinal bird, dressed in her dark red skirt, vest, and apron with a jacquard trim and wool stitching. Her sparkling brown eyes—behind small oval spectacles, perched on her nose—peer at her friends and family with curiosity and affection.

Each day, well before dawn, she rises from bed, tucks her smooth wooden crutch under her left arm, and washes her face with cold water poured from the pitcher at her dressing table. She combs her short dark hair until it is smooth and straight and pushes an olive-green band behind her ears to keep her hair in place while she works. Then Dahlia makes her way over to the castle. She adds wood to the coals of the night before and stokes the fires that heat the ovens, then sets out the items needed for the day's baking.

The castle kitchens are as neat as a pin, with a place for everything and everything in its place, which is just as Dahlia likes things to be.

Dahlia lives by the principle of mise en place, which means that one should precisely set out all the ingredients and tools one needs ahead of time and arrange the items so that everything is within arm's reach and ready to be used.

Arched alcoves ring the kitchen, holding shelves brimming with brightly colored cakes and other pastries for the king and his guests, loaves of crusty breads to sop up soups and stews, and all the supplies and tools that one could ever need. Sacks of flour and sugar; baskets of eggs;

wooden drawers of cinnamon, vanilla beans, cloves, and allspice; and crocks of fresh milk and butter all stand ready to be transformed into the loveliest pastries in the kingdom.

When the kitchens are humming along, warmed by the fires, with sweet scents wafting in the air accompanied by the happy clatter of spoons and measuring cups, Dahlia is certain there is no more wonderful place in the world.

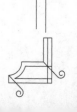

CHAPTER 1

Unfortunately, it was not one of those times.

"It's missing something!" exclaimed Dahlia, poking at the small pale-yellow cakes on the plate in front of her.

In her free time, Dahlia was trying to create the perfect confection for each of her dearest friends, and for Simon—the gentle giant of their group—she had envisioned the airy goodness of her grandmother's *jidangao*, a steamed sponge cake. Simon had been so sleepy lately that a cake as soft as a pillow seemed like the right fit for him.

But this was the third time she had attempted to make it, and it still didn't seem quite right.

Bazeema, one of Dahlia's other friends, appeared and took a small bite of cake. "Are you kidding? It's fantastic."

Dahlia jolted.

Bazeema was timid and had a habit of appearing at the oddest moments, seemingly out of nowhere. Dahlia could normally accept that the tall and slender Bazeema was capable of hiding many places, peering out with her large dark eyes. But the kitchens were Dahlia's territory—she knew every crack and crevice.

"Where did you come from?" asked Dahlia.

Bazeema shrugged vaguely. "Over there."

"I followed my grandmother's recipe to the last note," fretted Dahlia.

Her dear departed grandmother had left her a trove of recipes with copious instructions delicately handwritten in the margins.

For the meringue, whip the egg whites until the peaks are glossy and stiff!

Sift the flour, then measure!

Use the coarse brown sugar.

The notes were no substitute for being able to ask her grandmother questions, though. And the question Dahlia wanted to ask now was *Why doesn't this cake make me feel the way it did when you made it?*

Dahlia knew that the joy of food went beyond mere flavor. A cake could taste like the most perfectly ripened strawberry dipped into a fresh bowl of cream, but if it looked like, say, an old shoe, it changed how you experienced the dish. Even if you took a bite and loved it, there was a part of your brain that would say *yuck!* Taste, look, feeling—all these things were important, and Dahlia wanted the feeling the cake had given her when her grandmother had made it. She remembered that jidangao made her feel like she was wrapped in a blanket warmed by the fire.

Perhaps she was being too picky, but there was the not-so-small matter that Dahlia baked for King Magnifico! The kindest, smartest, most handsome king that ever lived.

Dahlia felt a particular conviction that every item she baked for the king in the king's kitchens should be perfect, not just because he had been the reason she had gotten the job as castle baker in the first place, but because food from the king's kitchens should be as wonderful as the king himself.

Take the King Magnifico cookies she had prepped earlier that morning. The recipe was not hers—it had been passed along to her from the castle baker before—but Dahlia made sure that every detail was perfect, right down to the exact shade of the king's captivating blue eyes.

"I just want . . ." she started to say, but Bazeema had vanished.

Dahlia counted the cakes—two more were missing.

"Hope you like them, Bazeema!" she said to the air. "Come again soon!"

Dahlia began picking up the bowls and spoons she had used for the jidangao, tidying her space so that she could begin her next bake of the day. There wasn't time to fret about Simon's cake any longer.

It was a wish-granting day, one of the most wonderful days in the kingdom. Anyone in Rosas who was over the age of eighteen and had given their wish to the king might have it granted at that day's ceremony.

Dahlia nursed a hope, even an expectation, that Saba Sabino would be chosen.

Sabino was the grandfather of her best friend, Asha, and he was turning one hundred years old that very day! Surely having a wish-granting ceremony on someone's hundredth birthday had to mean *something*. And Saba Sabino was one of the sweetest, gentlest souls in all of Rosas. Who could possibly be more deserving?

Dahlia couldn't wait to make a cake to celebrate when Sabino's wish was chosen.

As she began gathering the items to make that night's dessert for the king—a chocolate cake with layers of fresh raspberries—Dahlia began to wonder what the perfect cake for Saba Sabino might be, to celebrate the granting of a most long-awaited wish.

CHAPTER 2

Dahlia hummed while she sampled a taste of the batter she was mixing at the worktable. But as she looked up, she saw Asha racing through the doorway, with her pet goat, Valentino, prancing closely at her heels.

Valentino followed Asha everywhere. Asha's mother, Sakina, had even made him little pajamas to wear. But Dahlia didn't care how cute he was. Everything had a place in her kitchen—everything *except* curious baby goats who liked to climb all over, *especially* on Dahlia's proofing shelves, which were stacked with breakable bowls, precious bread starter, and rising pastries.

"Hello. Hi. Help me, best friend and honorary doctor of all things rational," Asha pleaded as she paced in circles around the worktable. "My interview is in one hour. I'm so nervous I could explode."

To Dahlia, it was impossible not to love Asha, and anyone who felt otherwise simply had not met Asha yet. With her bright smile and willingness to help anyone, at any time, Asha was the best person Dahlia knew. Dahlia also understood that she needed to help calm her friend. She reached for some lavender and rose petals and made sure the kettle was warm on the stove.

"Interview? What interview?" Dahlia played dumb as she started mixing herbs into a mug for her fretful friend.

"Dahlia!" Asha moaned as she grabbed the table, looking desperate.

"Ooooh, you mean the interview with our velvety sweet buttercream of a king." Dahlia sighed.

Her friend had applied to be the king's apprentice and made it to the final selection.

Dahlia nearly buzzed with excitement for her friend. She noticed that Asha's kirtle and surcoat—in pretty shades of lavender—were clean and pressed to perfection. Her beautiful dark braids framed her kind, open face, and she wore her coral necklace with matching earrings.

"Please don't say it like that." Asha cringed. She—unlike Dahlia—was not twitterpated with a crush on the king.

"My best friend, the king's apprentice. I'll be famous," Dahlia teased.

Asha was too distracted by her own worries to pay attention.

"I've forgotten how to talk. I have no words. Is my mouth drooping?"

She pulled the sides of her mouth down.

Dahlia smiled to herself. She loved her sweet, wonderful friend so much—even when she was needlessly worried and being silly. It was time to step in.

"Only when you pull it," she reassured. "Drink this. It's rose and lavender. Good for nerves."

Dahlia handed Asha the worn stoneware mug— its warmth leaving her own hands to comfort her friend's.

Asha took a sip of the tea, but her eyes were still wide with worry. "Quick, ask me an interview question."

"Okay," Dahlia said, playing along, as though Asha hadn't already had her ask what probably amounted to *one thousand* practice questions leading up to this day. "What's your weakness?"

"Weakness? Uhhhh, I get irrational when I'm nervous," Asha replied.

"No. No." Dahlia shook her head, correcting her friend. *"You care too much."*

It was true. Asha cared for *everyone.* Every

friend. Every neighbor. Every person in their community. Every visitor who traveled from far and wide just to catch a glimpse of their magical kingdom. She might have been younger than many of the other candidates, but Asha was one of the most thoughtful and considerate people in all of Rosas.

"I do?" Asha seemed puzzled. "Is that a weakness?"

"That's why it's perfect." Dahlia winked. "You're welcome."

"Oh, I think I'm going to be sick." Asha grimaced.

Dahlia raised her eyebrows in alarm and nervously pulled her bowl of batter farther away from her friend.

"This is a kitchen. Don't even joke," Dahlia warned.

But she saw that her friend really did look the worse for wear.

"Just relax," she said, returning her voice to the

soothing tone she knew Asha needed. "You're sur-rounded by friends."

Asha looked around. They were not, in fact, surrounded by anyone at the moment.

Dahlia knew just the trick to fix that, though.

She lifted a cloth to reveal a tray full of King Magnifico cookies on the table. Even then, she couldn't help scanning them to make sure each one perfectly represented their handsome ruler.

Is the nose off on one?

Right on cue, the smell of the freshly baked cookies now wafting from the worktable roused Simon from where he was slumbering on a sack of flour in the corner of the kitchen.

"Mmm, cookies?" he asked with a yawn.

Simon reminded Dahlia of an ox, big and strong-shouldered. He had turned eighteen a few months prior and given his wish to the king. He had always been a little tired, but now it was more pronounced. It was almost like he was half-asleep

most of the time (and fully asleep the rest of the time).

As Simon stifled another yawn, four of their other friends dropped what they were working on to race to the cookie tray.

"Cookies!" Hal called happily. She was the beekeeper of Rosas. Hal brightened any room just by entering it and was almost always abuzz with joy. And her honey was unrivaled throughout the kingdom—so much so, in fact, Dahlia even kept a jar of it in her pocket.

You never know when you might need a dab of something sweet, she would explain to anyone who gave her a strange look when she pulled out the jar. *It goes where I go.*

"Look out!" Safi sniffed as he made his way over. Safi cared for the castle chickens (he sometimes had one perched on his head like a feathery hat), and it seemed as though something or other was always making him sneeze, which turned his already red nose even redder. He was very lanky, so when he sneezed, his whole body jerked backward like a marionette yanked on a string.

"Mine!" Gabo declared as he dashed for the cookies. He was a squat boy with a permanent frown. If there was something even remotely unpleasant to say, Gabo thought of it and said it.

"Cookies!" echoed Dario. But unlike the other friends, he ran *past* the worktable and out of the room entirely. Everyone turned to look.

Where is he going? Dahlia wondered.

Then they all shrugged—after all, Dario wasn't the *brightest* candle of the bunch. They all loved him, though. He was an integral member of their little crew, and he always kept them smiling.

The friends resumed fighting over the cookies. Gabo—being on the shorter side of things—got blocked out of the way but managed to get a hand through just as Dahlia remembered to warn Safi that he was allergic to this particular recipe.

"Careful, Safi! They're lemon—"

But it was too late.

Safi sneezed right onto the entire tray of cookies—and Gabo's hand, too!

"No! Ahhh," Gabo wailed. "Life is so unfair!"

"You can have mine, Gabo," Bazeema said softly. She had once again appeared out of nowhere.

"Bazeema! Argh!" Gabo startled. "Where did you come from?"

"I've been here the whole time."

Dahlia made a mental note to check the kitchens more thoroughly for nooks to hide in.

Maybe a butter cookie would be the appropriate treat to represent Bazeema, Dahlia thought. *Since they completely melt away in your mouth. . . .*

Bazeema smiled shyly as she held out one of the cookies that none of them had noticed her take before Safi had sneezed on them.

Gabo didn't stop scowling, but he took the King Magnifico cookie from Bazeema and bit the head off—a little too aggressively, in Dahlia's opinion. She couldn't help wincing.

"Oh, take mine, too. I can't eat," Asha said, wide-eyed, as she gulped her tea.

"Oh, right, your interview with the king." Gabo smirked. "Don't worry, we'll be here for you when you fail."

"Gabo!" Hal chided.

"What?" Gabo replied matter-of-factly. "Most people fail at everything."

Dahlia shook her head. *Would it hurt Gabo to say something nice?*

Just then Dario walked back through the door to the kitchens.

"Oh, *there* are the cookies!" he exclaimed as he reached for one.

"Dario, look out!" Dahlia warned. "Safi sneezed on those."

"Oh. Thanks," Dario replied as he ate the cookie anyway, unfazed.

Gabo shuddered as they all tried to ignore what had just happened.

"Anywaaaay," Gabo said, turning back to Asha.

Dahlia recognized the stubborn look in his eye. Gabo was like a dog with a bone when he had a certain idea—and she could tell that he was not going to let Asha off the hook about her interview with the king.

CHAPTER 3

"Not that I blame you for trying to cheat the system," Gabo said, scoffing.

Dahlia felt herself getting hot. *How dare he speak to Asha that way!*

But Asha kept her cool. "What? I'm not trying to cheat anything," she replied.

"Come on, everyone knows that the king's apprentices get their wishes granted," said Gabo, pointing an accusatory finger up at Asha and narrowing his eyes. "And usually their *family's* wishes, too."

Gabo sounded almost smug.

Dahlia waited for Asha to defend herself and deny Gabo's accusation. Did Asha look a little sheepish? Dahlia dove in to help instead.

"Not always!" said Dahlia as she tried to think of an example, but she came up empty.

"Well, maybe always."

Ugh, Dahlia groaned to herself. *There is really nothing worse than seeing that in all his naysaying, Gabo might have a point.*

"Your saba's a hundred today and still waiting," Gabo continued.

Dahlia did not like his tone.

"Tonight's his night," said Hal, but in a nice way.

Ah, so I'm not the only one who thinks so! Dahlia smiled to herself.

Bazeema chimed in, too. "I can feel it. Everybody thinks so!"

"Ignore him," Safi added, giving Gabo a scowl.

Except for Gabo—and Simon, who was asleep again—all the friends smiled warmly at Asha, thinking of Saba Sabino. Then Gabo spoiled the moment.

"Not to mention the fact that you're also turning eighteen—" Gabo added, like a detective laying out evidence.

"Happy birthday!" Dario interrupted.

"In a few months," Gabo clarified for Dario with an exasperated sigh before turning back to Asha. "And when you give your wish to the king, you don't want to have to end up like Simon here."

Hearing his name must have woken Simon again. "What's wrong with Simon here?" he asked groggily.

"It's not your fault," Gabo explained. "Everyone becomes boring after they give their wish."

"Have I become boring?" Simon asked, sitting up. Dahlia could see a look of hurt in his eyes. "Do you all think that?"

The friends tried to answer as politely as possible—while Safi just sneezed to avoid the question entirely.

"Not boring, no, just . . ." Asha's voice trailed off.

"More peaceful," Hal suggested.

"Calmer," said Dahlia, having thought of the kindest synonym for *sleepy* as possible.

"More . . . content?" added Bazeema.

Simon's face fell. He knew his friends. He could tell when they weren't being honest with him. And Dahlia could tell it was upsetting him to hear that they thought he had changed—and not for the better—since he'd given his wish. He touched his own arm, as if checking to see he hadn't given an actual part of himself away.

Thankfully, Asha spoke up for the rest of them, doing what she always did best to reassure him.

"Simon, don't worry." She smiled. "You're still you, and I bet you get your wish granted really soon."

It was a nice moment.

Too bad Gabo had to foul the air like old cheese.

"Unlike your poor old saba, who's still waiting," he said snidely.

Dahlia had had enough. But before she could step in, Asha took matters into her own hands to quiet their grumpy friend. She snatched up a handful of flour and blew it into Gabo's face. The air became hazy with the white powder as Gabo and the others coughed and sputtered.

"Asha?" someone asked from across the room, through the cloudy scene. The voice was low, regal, soft but powerful.

"The queen." Asha gasped.

"Oh my goodness. Quickly," Dahlia instructed the others. The friends scrambled as they tried to form a line, curtsying and bowing before Queen Amaya of Rosas.

"This is so exciting," Hal squealed.

"Don't sneeze. Don't *sneeze!*" Safi urged himself.

"We're so embarrassing," whispered Gabo through clenched teeth.

Even Valentino the goat seemed to perk up with respect.

If Queen Amaya heard these comments, she did not let on.

The king held so much of Rosas' attention with his wish-granting ceremonies that it was easy to overlook the queen, who was quieter. But looking at her now, Dahlia took in her presence. The queen held herself with poise, her posture not unlike a dancer's, and she seemed to see everything.

"Cookie?" Dario offered as he held out one of the sneeze-covered King Magnifico cookies for the queen. Dahlia almost passed out from horror on the spot. She put her hand on top of Dario's, trying to lower his offering.

"No, thank you," the queen replied, and Dahlia

breathed a sigh of relief as she thanked her lucky stars.

Queen Amaya turned to Asha, who was trying to wave away the cloud of flour still lingering in the air.

"Asha, the king is ready for you," the queen said.

"Now? Am I late? I thought I—" Asha brushed the flour from her clothes.

"You're fine," said the queen reassuringly. "The last interview—"

The queen's comment was interrupted by howls from out in the hallway.

"It was a disaster!" sobbed the howling voice's owner.

"Finished early." Queen Amaya diplomatically ended her sentence. "Shall we?"

With that, she turned and walked out the door.

"Oh. Okay." Asha's shoulders rose and fell as

she took a deep breath. "I'm ready," she announced.

Dahlia felt a surge of pride for her friend.

Then Asha turned to Dahlia.

"I am *so* not ready," she whispered.

Dahlia tried to come up with some last-minute advice.

"You're fine. Just don't touch anything, don't forget to curtsy, and tell him I love him." She was close to babbling now.

Asha did a double take.

"I'm kidding," said Dahlia hastily. *"Do not* tell him that."

Asha just nodded, turned, and—still wide-eyed—followed the queen out the door.

"Bye. Don't get your hopes up!" Gabo called after her.

Dahlia really had to wonder where all of Gabo's negativity came from. It was so hard not to be equally rude sometimes, like now, when she wanted him to be quiet. Luckily, Valentino made their feelings clear, letting out a long, disgusted *baaaaaaa* at Gabo to voice his disapproval sharply.

Dahlia silently agreed.

It was bad when even a goat knew you were being rude!

CHAPTER 4

"Do not touch that!"

"Stay away from there!"

"Can't you just sit still?"

Watching Valentino while Asha was at her interview was no easy task. It felt like her friend had been gone for hours, though if Dahlia was honest, it was probably only fifteen minutes. In that short amount of time, though, Valentino had managed to get into all sorts of trouble. He'd climbed and subsequently toppled from various shelves, tables, and anything else he could reach. He had left a trail of frosting hoofprints across the kitchen and eaten an entire basket of apples Dahlia had set aside for a pie. She had only looked away for a minute!

Valentino hopped from a stool to a bench where Dahlia had set the king's cake to cool so she could cut it into layers and then frost it. The goat brushed against the cake stand, making it wobble.

"Noooo!" cried Dahlia.

She quickly held the cake steady as Valentino stumbled off the bench and popped back up as though nothing had happened. He went over to a nearby crock of cream and got ready to dip his head in to take a drink. Dahlia caught him just in time.

He can't help himself, Dahlia told herself. *He's a goat. He doesn't understand what's happening.*

Why on earth did Asha's family have to get a

goat? Didn't Asha remember the last time there had been a goat in the kitchens?

Or maybe that was precisely why she had gotten Valentino.

The thought made Dahlia smile.

"Would you like to hear a story?" she asked Valentino, half joking. But to her astonishment, the little goat looked up at her and seemed to nod.

Maybe he understood more than she gave him credit for. Dahlia picked up a handful of carrots, sat down in one of the wooden chairs, and beckoned Valentino to her. The little goat hopped up into her lap, and as she slowly fed him carrots, she started to tell him one of her favorite memories.

"Many years ago," Dahlia began, "before I knew Asha, I was invited to the castle kitchens. . . ."

* ✦ *

Dahlia had received a note from the castle welcoming her grandmother and her to visit.

Word of Dahlia's grandmother's baking—accomplished with the help of her talented young granddaughter, or *niuniu*, as Dahlia's grandmother liked to call her—had apparently reached the king. Dahlia's grandmother had fallen ill the day before they were set to visit the castle kitchens, but she urged Dahlia to go without her. It would have been rude not to accept the invitation.

"You can do it," said her grandmother tenderly. "Just remember, bake with love."

Dahlia nodded, feeling the weight of her assignment, and then made her way to the castle, her apron tied tightly around her waist. She remembered knocking on the huge door, wondering if anyone could hear her through the thick, heavy wood.

"Eh?" A man in a large white apron opened the door and looked around, appearing to see no one. Then he looked down. "You!" he said to Dahlia.

"Me!" Dahlia agreed.

"You are the young baker we have heard so much about?" he asked. "I thought you would be older."

"I am ten years old," said Dahlia firmly.

"Very well, come in, come in." The baker sighed. "It's really not a good day for you to visit. And I thought your grandmother was supposed to come, too? I don't have time to babysit. I have a celebration to prepare desserts for, but the queen has requested cinnamon-sugar cookies for a picnic this afternoon."

Dahlia drew herself up.

"I do *not* need to be babysat," she said. "I came to bake."

She pointed to her apron as proof.

"*And* I know how to make cinnamon-sugar cookies."

The soft chewy treats had been one of the first things she had learned to make with her grandmother.

The baker raised a bushy, skeptical eyebrow.

"That would be very useful," he admitted. "That way, I could focus on the cakes for the king's celebration."

"How many cookies do you need?" asked Dahlia.

"Two dozen ought to do it," said the baker.

Then he shook his head as if remembering that he was asking a child to help in the royal kitchens. To make cookies for the queen!

"Are you sure you know how to make them? Will you need help with the oven?"

"I know how to use the oven." Dahlia tried not to sound annoyed with his skepticism. "I'll need flour, salt, butter, sugar, eggs, a vanilla bean, and cinnamon sticks, of course. I prefer Ceylon cinnamon sticks to grind if you have them."

"What is this!" said the baker, baffled. "You know there are different kinds of cinnamon? Not even I knew that until I was much older."

"Of course," said Dahlia. "Ceylon cinnamon is sweeter. My grandmother taught me that."

Dahlia was not showing off. It was simply a fact. Her grandmother had taught her many things— like how to baste her pastries with egg wash so a bright sheen would develop in the oven; to roll small chunks of chocolate in flour so they would not fall to the bottom of a batter; and to use a thin string pulled taut to cut a cake into even layers.

"Well," said the baker, relaxing a little bit. "Perhaps this will all be fine."

He said this as much to himself as to Dahlia.

"If you do a good job, perhaps you can have my job when you are older."

Dahlia's heart swelled. Baking for King Magnifico was a dream for her, even at the young age of ten.

"You won't be sorry," she promised.

.⁺✦⁺⁺.

Dahlia made the cookies without incident.

The baker tasted one and pronounced it "exceptional."

By the time the cookies had fully cooled, Dahlia had been left alone in the kitchens while the baker went to supervise the arrangement of the desserts in the grand ballroom for the celebration that evening.

Cookies for a picnic need a basket, Dahlia decided.

She rummaged around the shelves until she found a small basket and a pretty linen napkin. She laid the cloth in the basket, nestled the cookies inside, and allowed herself the satisfaction of sniffing them one last time.

"I suppose I should wait here until the baker comes back," said Dahlia.

She made sure everything was cleaned and put away properly and then allowed herself to close her eyes for a moment to rest. It had been such an exciting morning.

"I'll listen for the baker," she told herself. "As soon as I hear his footsteps, I'll wake up so he won't think I'm being lazy."

She must have dozed off longer than she intended, but the sound of a door creaking woke her. She shot up, looking around for the baker and then the basket of cookies to show him. But she did not see either.

What she saw was a goat, holding the handle of the basket of cookies in its mouth.

Dahlia shook her head a little to wake up.

"I must be dreaming," she told herself.

But then she noticed the rectangular shape of the goat's pupils, the brass bell tied around its neck that jingled when it moved, and the distinctly goaty smell it exuded.

This was real.

The goat looked at her, let out one sharp bleat, and then bounded out the door with the basket of cookies.

"Stop that goat!" shouted Dahlia, following after it.

What if the baker came back and discovered that Dahlia had left *and* there were no cookies? There would be no way that she would ever become the castle baker. She had to get those cookies back, and quickly!

The goat skipped down the lane and then jumped over a low stone wall. Dahlia leaned over the wall and spotted the bleating thief heading toward a green space bounded on one side by a reflecting pond. A girl with long dark braids was sitting with her family on a blanket under a tree.

"Please!" called Dahlia. "Please stop that goat, or at least slow him down until I get there."

The girl with the dark braids immediately stood up and waved to Dahlia.

"I'll do my best," she said.

She crouched down and began walking toward the goat.

Dahlia made her way down a few steps cut through the low wall. The girl had kept the goat from running farther away from Dahlia by blocking off one path. The animal was hemmed in between the girl and Dahlia, with the pond on the other side.

"I need to get that basket back from the goat," Dahlia explained. "It has cookies for the queen."

"Cookies for the queen!" exclaimed the girl. "This calls for emergency measures."

"Thank you . . ." Dahlia paused, realizing that she didn't know the girl's name. "I'm Dahlia, like the flower."

"Asha," said the girl. "We can get to know more about each other later. Right now, we need to focus on this goat!"

Asha held out her arms and walked toward the goat, trying to get it to back up toward Dahlia. The goat suddenly jumped sideways, sending the basket swaying so hard that the cookies nearly fell out.

"Whoa!" yelped Dahlia. "I can't have broken cookies!"

"Oh, yes, of course," said Asha.

The two girls managed to corner the goat in a smaller space with the pond on one side and a fence and a tree on the other. The goat would either have to come toward them or go into the pond.

"Goats can't swim, can they?" asked Asha.

"I'm not sure," said Dahlia. "At least goats don't climb trees."

And then, as if to prove Dahlia wrong, the goat leapt into the tree!

"I regret that statement," said Dahlia with a groan, watching the goat begin to climb the tree. "Also, I have a lot to learn about goats."

She watched the goat climb higher.

"Please don't drop the basket!"

Asha tucked a braid behind one ear, thinking.

"We need to offer something as a trade. Something of equal value to the goat."

"What?" asked Dahlia. She wasn't sure she was hearing correctly. "You want to negotiate?"

"Ne-*goat*-tiate," said Asha, laughing. "Get it?"

Dahlia laughed in spite of herself.

"Now I know something about you, Asha. You make terrible puns. But your idea isn't bad. I guess it's worth a shot." Dahlia dug her hand into her pocket but came up empty.

"I spent all morning in the kitchens and I don't have a speck of food on me," she lamented.

"Let me ask my saba," said Asha. "Keep an eye on the goat."

She walked back to the blanket and chatted with an old man. After a moment, the man removed the straw hat from his head and handed it to Asha.

"I don't think goats wear hats," said Dahlia doubtfully. "Their heads are kind of small."

"Not to wear! To eat!" Asha waved the hat up and down, giggling. "We think the goat will like the straw."

She held the hat up toward the goat.

"You don't want those cookies, do you? Not when you can have this nice crunchy hat!"

The goat stopped climbing, watching Asha.

"Come on," she coaxed. "It's such a delicious hat!"

She held the hat up.

"Look at this nice big hat. So much more food than that little basket!"

The girl pretended to take a big bite of the hat.

"Oh, so yummy! This hat is delicious! It's like, um . . ."

She turned to Dahlia.

"Quick! What do goats like?"

"You're asking me?!" said Dahlia. "I was the one who thought goats couldn't climb trees!"

Then Dahlia had a terrible thought.

What if the goat started eating the basket?

Fortunately, at that moment, the goat decided that it *did* want the hat instead. It opened its mouth and dropped the basket as it reached down for the hat.

Dahlia felt like she was watching the basket fall in slow motion. The basket hit a branch and tipped slightly. It hit another branch and tipped in another direction.

"Oh no!" cried Asha.

If I try to catch the basket, thought Dahlia, *I might just miss and tip them over. But if the basket hits the ground, the cookies will all break.*

Suddenly, she knew what to do.

"Quick, grab the hem of my apron and pull it toward you," she directed Asha.

Asha did so, and the apron formed a large pouch just in time for the basket to land softly in the middle.

Dahlia exhaled.

"Oh my goodness!" said Asha. "We saved them!"

"Let's check," said Dahlia. She lifted the cloth.

"Only one cookie broke! That should be okay."

Dahlia silently thanked her grandmother for teaching her to always bake a few extra of whatever she made, just in case.

"Want to share this broken one?" Dahlia asked, offering half the cookie to Asha. "It's the least I can do to say thank you!"

"I never turn down a cookie," said Asha, taking a bite. "That was brilliant, by the way. I didn't know aprons could be so handy."

"Normally they're good for keeping clothes clean," said Dahlia, chewing on her half of the cookie. "But this works, too!"

She looked up to see Asha devouring her last bite.

"That was the best cookie I've ever had!" Asha exclaimed. "No wonder you're baking for the queen!"

Dahlia shrugged, suddenly embarrassed.

"I owe you one," she said.

"Good job, girls!" called the old man.

Asha smiled.

"It was mostly Dahlia! This is Dahlia!"

She turned to Dahlia and gestured back at the people.

"That's my mother, my father, and my grandfather, Saba Sabino."

Dahlia looked up at the goat, still in the tree. The goat was watching them as it chewed on the hat.

"May I bring Sabino a new hat sometime soon?" asked Dahlia. "I don't think that one is going to be a hat much longer."

The goat had nearly finished the brim.

"You *could* bring him a hat," Asha replied, smiling. "Or some of these incredible cookies!"

"I'll bring over a batch tomorrow," said Dahlia. "I need to get back to the castle now and give these to the queen."

"I was kidding about the hat and the cookies,"

said Asha. "You don't owe us anything. But you should come over and visit! We'll find more trouble to get into."

"This was enough trouble for me!" Dahlia replied, laughing, as she started to make her way back toward the castle.

"Fine, call it fun, then!" Asha hollered across the grass, beaming as she waved goodbye. "Because that's what this really was. Fun!"

All the way back to the kitchens, young Dahlia kept replaying in her head what had happened. A goat had stolen her cookies! She had nearly lost them after having to follow said goat around what felt like half the castle grounds! She was hot and sweaty, but there she was, smiling. As she stepped through the door to the kitchens, the baker turned and looked at her.

"Eh! Where have you been? The queen is asking for those cookies!"

"I, uh . . ." Dahlia realized that saying she had been chasing after a goat who had stolen her basket of cookies was so ridiculous it might sound like a lie. What could she say?

"A friend was helping me with something," she said, handing the basket of cookies over to the baker.

As soon as she said the words, she realized they were truer than true.

She had found a friend.

And they were still friends, years later.

While Dahlia reminisced, Valentino had crawled into her lap. Now he was nearly asleep. Dahlia lowered her head to whisper in Valentino's ear.

"That's how Asha and I became best friends. And I thought we were done with goats, until you came along!"

She paused and gave the baby goat a little hug.

"But I guess goats aren't *so* bad."

Outside, a trumpet sounded. Dahlia started.

The wish-granting ceremony! With Asha's interview and so much going on, she'd nearly forgotten.

She led Valentino outside, joining their other friends for what was sure to be Sabino's big moment. She couldn't wait to see his wish come true!

CHAPTER 5

Wish-granting days were always the best days in Rosas.

As everyone gathered in the arena next to the castle, cheery trumpets and rat-a-tat drums played lively music, matching the energy of the awaiting crowd.

A wish!

Someone (probably Saba Sabino!) was going to get their wish!

Even though dusk was nearing, the sun seemed

to shine brighter in anticipation of the ceremony. People chattered and laughed. Some were even dancing, they felt that joyful. Everyone kept glancing toward the stage a few feet above them. That was where the king would perform the ceremony.

Dahlia found Asha's mother, Sakina, and dear Sabino. Asha had sadly lost her father only a year after she and Dahlia had become friends. Their family had been through so much, it would be such a gift for Saba Sabino to receive his wish.

Then King Magnifico stepped out onto the stage and the crowd erupted into cheers.

With a sweeping gesture, he sent arcs of dazzling, colorful magic over the crowd, drawing sounds of admiration from the people.

"Are you ready, Rosas?!" he boomed.

Even though she had seen King Magnifico more times than she could count, his appearance still took Dahlia's breath away. He was a tall man, with broad shoulders that seemed to bear the weight of his reign easily. His thick hair and beard, always finely coiffed, had begun to silver, but that only made him more distinguished.

It was his eyes, though, that most people remarked upon.

Poets in Rosas had tried and failed to describe their depths and how they affected those he gazed upon. They were richer than the sky on a sunny day, but brighter than the ocean's blue. The gardeners of Rosas tried to propagate their blue flowers—thistles, irises, delphiniums, and hydrangeas—to match his eyes, but they shook their heads in disappointment at every attempt. None could match the exact shade. (Though Dahlia was sure her King Magnifico cookies back in the kitchen captured the color almost to a tee.)

Queen Amaya sat onstage behind the king.

What a lucky queen, thought Dahlia.

She soon became distracted by the excited flush in Sabino's cheeks, though. Surely today would be his day. It would be so perfect, with its being his hundredth birthday. And Asha was probably going to be the king's apprentice. Who else could it be?

Dahlia leaned over to speak to Saba Sabino.

"I was just telling Valentino about how I met Asha."

If the old man thought it was strange to talk to a goat, he didn't show it. His eyes crinkled up at the corners.

"I remember that like it was yesterday!"

"I think I still owe you a hat," said Dahlia, laughing.

"Not at all," said Sakina, squeezing her arm.

Sabino nodded.

"You are like family to us," he said. "You bring so much love to our home. We are the lucky ones."

"I feel the same way," said Dahlia, her eyes turning misty with how much she cared for them. How they had become part of her *own* family.

Then Dahlia saw Asha onstage, too, sitting next to the queen!

"It's Asha!" she cried, pointing. "She made it!"

"Made *what?*" Sakina asked.

Oh, that was so typically Asha, to not tell her family about her big interview just in case things didn't go her way.

"She was . . ." Dahlia hesitated. Was it her information to share? She met Sakina's expectant gaze and knew she didn't really have a choice.

"Interviewing to be the king's apprentice . . ." Dahlia finished sheepishly.

"Ha! I knew she was up to something." Sakina laughed in response as she looked with pride at her daughter on stage. "That's my baby!"

The king's voice carried over them again.

"Another beautiful night in my kingdom," said King Magnifico, his voice ringing out effortlessly across the crowd. "So good to see you, good to be seen."

Dahlia would never admit this to anyone—all right, anyone besides Asha—but if there were such a thing as a handsome voice, King Magnifico had one. His voice sounded like a cello, low and rich, and when he spoke, everyone wanted to listen.

She sighed, willing the foggy clouds of her crush on the king to temporarily scatter. She needed to focus on this big moment for Asha, Sabino, and Sakina!

Asha looked over to where they were all standing, and her friends and family waved back and cheered with excitement. Surely having Asha onstage meant that she had been selected as the king's apprentice.

Dahlia was thrilled.

Her amazing, kind friend was going to be the apprentice to their wonderful king, and Saba Sabino was going to get his wish on his hundredth birthday! What a lucky day for them all!

But then, as Dahlia looked more closely, she realized that Asha's expression was not joyous. Her head sank so that her chin nearly touched her chest. Her mouth did not curve into her usual bright smile but stayed closed and small, in a straight line. And her eyebrows drew together with concern.

Why would Asha look sad? Dahlia wondered. *Maybe I'm seeing things. Maybe Asha is just trying to look serious and grown-up in front of everyone in Rosas. That would be more than understandable. . . .*

"First things first," said the king, interrupting Dahlia's thoughts. "We have two new citizens ready to give their wishes!"

The crowd cheered again.

Although wish *giving* did not receive as much attention as wish *granting*, it was just as important. Wish giving meant that a person entrusted the king with their deepest, most heartfelt desire. Once they gave their wish, they no longer remembered it—or, as the saying went, they could "forget without regret." They no longer had to worry about their wish, since it was safely in the hands of their king.

A man and a woman new to Rosas, Esteban and Helena, stepped onto the stage. They smiled nervously. King Magnifico must have reassured them, as they soon raised their hands, palms facing upward.

The king swirled his own palms, creating a magic energy, then clasped their outstretched hands. The crowd fell silent, watching the magic before them, as Helena's and Esteban's eyes grew wide with awe.

As soon as King Magnifico touched the couple's hands, a glow began to emanate from inside their chests, over their hearts. The light moved, rushing down their arms, and then suddenly appeared in their cupped palms, clear and delicate, like bubbles.

Magnifico quickly took them from their hands, and Helena and Esteban seemed to falter a bit. Their faces fell as the emanating glow disappeared.

"Forget without regret!" chanted the crowd.

Dahlia noticed that the king then glanced back at Asha, as if to make sure she was paying attention now that she was his apprentice. Asha looked at the king and then turned to gaze across the crowd. Dahlia could have sworn that she looked straight at them again, her friends and family, but her face remained blank.

The king rubbed his hands together as the couple left the stage, holding on to each other. It was time for the main event.

CHAPTER 6

"Okay, then," said King Magnifico. "Who is ready to have their wish granted?!"

The crowd responded with wild cheers. Dahlia looked over at Sabino, who was holding hands with Sakina. She wished with her whole heart that she could capture this happy moment to share with Asha. But Asha would have her own joyous memory!

King Magnifico continued.

"Now, I have been challenged today to take

a chance and try something new." He turned to look at Asha again. "Thank you, Asha."

Dahlia's heart thumped in her chest.

The king had actually said Asha's name onstage, in front of everyone! Dahlia felt as though she might faint just from being so close to the king's splendor through Asha.

The king turned his attention back to the crowd, smiling warmly.

"And it is with clarity and an open heart full of love that I grant today's wish to someone who has very patiently waited long enough!"

Long enough! thought Dahlia. *That means Sabino. It can only be Sabino!*

The people around her seemed to echo Dahlia's thoughts.

"Sabino!"

"It's got to be Sabino!"

"It's his turn."

"He must be so happy!"

Asha was looking at her saba from the stage; he

smiled back lovingly. But Dahlia saw something in her best friend's eyes that confused her. . . .

Is that . . . despair? Dahlia wondered.

The king's voice rang out again.

"Sania Osman!" the king declared.

For a moment, Dahlia was convinced she had misheard. How could the king have mispronounced Sabino's name like that?

But no.

"Where is Sania? There she is. Come on up, Sania," urged the king. "Please come forward."

Dahlia heard a woman squeal.

"He said Sania? It's me? It's me. It's me!"

Then she heard the excited shouts of Sania's family and friends. But Dahlia could only look at Saba Sabino.

Of course, for Sabino to be disappointed would be to reveal that he had expected to be chosen. The humble old man would never admit to such a thing, but he closed his eyes as Sakina wrapped her arms around him.

How could this have happened? Dahlia wondered.

Around them, people glanced at the old man pityingly. Shock and confusion hung in the air as thick as fog. Dahlia looked back toward the stage. Asha's eyes were closed, her mouth still tight and small.

The woman scrambled through the crowd, trying to get to the stage. In her elation, she tripped and fell, and the people around her laughed and helped pick her up, patting her on the back, sharing their congratulations. They were already distracted from Sabino's disappointment.

"Coming through," Sania called. "Thank you, it's just so exciting!"

She rushed up the stairs to join King Magnifico, her face turned up toward him like a flower to sunlight.

"Sania Osman! I mean it when I say it truly is my great pleasure to grant your heart's desire," declared the king.

He held Sania's wish aloft, letting it glint in the

setting sun, allowing the moment to build. The crowd roared with approval as the king waved his hands. The wish swirled and then grew, encircling Sania, as the king granted her deepest hope:

"TO SEW THE MOST BEAUTIFUL DRESSES IN ALL THE LANDS!"

"My wish has come true!" cried Sania.

Dahlia tried to feel happy for her. The crowd around them certainly was.

"This is thrilling!"

"So wonderful!"

If the king chose Sania, he must have his reasons, right? she reminded herself. *The king knows best whose wish to grant.*

And whose wish to deny.

But her heart was breaking for Sabino, Sakina, and Asha.

"Poor Saba," said Dahlia as she watched Sakina give him a hug.

"He's waited so long," Simon said with a sigh.

"See, never ever get your hopes up," Gabo

added in an I-told-you-so voice, though Dahlia thought he looked disappointed, too.

"I'm so sorry, Saba," said Sakina, rubbing his arm.

Up on the stage, Sania waved to the crowd.

"Let's hear it for Sania Osman!" cheered the king.

Dahlia watched as Queen Amaya stood up and gave Sania a hug. Meanwhile, the king leaned over to Asha, saying something only those onstage could hear. The queen turned her head toward them, her mouth opening in surprise. It was clear that the king had said something to Asha that the queen was not expecting.

Asha grew smaller in her seat, shrinking in the king's shadow.

Then Dahlia saw Magnifico walk off the stage with a confused-looking Queen Amaya following, leaving Asha behind.

Something wasn't right.

Maybe Asha had *not* gotten the job. She had

been onstage the whole time, but the king had never introduced her as his new apprentice. That would explain Asha's sadness, and maybe why Saba had not gotten his wish.

Dahlia shook her head, trying to clear her thoughts. She wished Asha were next to her so she could comfort her—and find out what was really going on.

CHAPTER 7

After the wish-granting ceremony, the crowd broke up into smaller pockets of people heading back to their homes. Dahlia watched as Sakina and Sabino walked away, slower and sadder than she had ever seen them. Then she turned to go to her own home. Maybe she could make them something—a sweet loaf with Sabino and Asha's favorite dried fruits—to cheer them up.

Dahlia's wish was to become the best baker. Some people thought she already was the best baker, because she baked for the king. But Dahlia felt deep down that *truly* being the best would feel different. Her pastries would never leave her with that feeling she'd had earlier with Simon's cake, the irksome suspicion that even the tiniest something was not exactly right. And if her wish were granted, her parents would be so proud! She would also be honoring everything her grandmother had taught her in their hours spent together gathering ingredients, preparing everything perfectly, and enduring the heat of the oven.

Still, Dahlia often wondered what it would mean to give her wish to the king. As much as she admired King Magnifico, she could not imagine what it would be like to not have this wish inside of her.

Once you gave your wish to the king, you forgot its existence.

Forget without regret.

Would she feel like the same person?

Simon had been acting a bit strange since he gave his wish to the king. He slept more frequently, often dozing off at a moment's notice. Even when he was awake, he didn't seem to want to do the same things he had once enjoyed.

Before he gave his wish to the king for safe-keeping, when someone suggested riding horses or spending time outside, Simon was often the first to say yes, and he had loved using his size and strength to help his friends navigate the terrain or climb over boulders. Now Simon just rolled over and went to sleep.

And yet, giving her wish to King Magnifico meant that she would get to stand near him and bask in his splendidness. More than his good looks, Dahlia appreciated the king's care and attention, like the way he had sent for her and her grand-mother to bake in the castle that day all those years before, which had led to Dahlia meeting her best friend and extended chosen family. And the way he had recognized her gift for baking, giving her the job of castle baker—even at her young age of sixteen—when the role became available.

Surely not every king took care of his subjects with so much consideration!

Not everyone is so lucky to entrust their wish to such a good and kind ruler, Dahlia reminded herself.

But then she had a horrible thought.

What if, when I give my wish, I stop thinking about baking?

Dahlia couldn't imagine that was even possible. She loved *everything* about what she did in the kitchens, whether imagining dazzling cakes of delight or turning out chewy loaves of bread with crackling brown crusts. She loved the smell of pastries coming out of the oven at dawn, the sight of bright yellow egg yolks in a bowl, and the rhythmic thump of kneading bread.

Baking was how Dahlia told the people around her that she loved them. She also loved thinking of the "how" of it all. Like figuring out which pastry would be best for a Sunday morning breakfast— Dahlia thought of how a warm scallion bun, fresh from the steamer, settled her father's upset stomach. And what birthday cake might bring a friend the most delight? Even a grouch like Gabo smiled at the sight of his favorite (or as he said, "least disliked") dark chocolate cake.

I have plenty of time to decide, Dahlia told herself.

She had two more years, to be exact, until she turned eighteen and could give the king her wish. She yawned. It had been quite a long day. She lit a candle and then sat on her bed with a book she was reading (or re-reading), *Favorite Pastries of Rosas.*

She was just getting to the section on biscuits when, out of the corner of her eye, she noticed a soft, rolling light against the inky blue night through her window. She looked up just in time for the light to fill her vision and warm her face.

Suddenly, Dahlia was full of memories, memories of love and light and beauty.

Picking flowers for a bouquet for her mother.

Looking for pretty seashells on the beach.

Baking with her grandmother.

Going on a picnic with her friends and taking the warm crusty baguettes she had just pulled from the oven.

Meeting Asha for the first time.

Dahlia sighed and hugged herself, as if to hold all the memories inside of her.

CHAPTER 8

The next day, in the kitchens, the light was all anyone could talk about. The friends gathered around the table where Dahlia baked—well, Gabo, Hal, and Safi were eating some of her cookies, while Simon was asleep with his head on the table. They hadn't seen a sign of Dario yet, and no one knew where Bazeema was, per usual.

Asha was not there, either. Dahlia felt a pang for her friend and wondered how she, Sabino, and Sakina were doing after the disappointing wish ceremony the night before.

"Even *you* have to admit, Gabo, that light last night felt amazing," Hal said.

That was Hal, always trying to draw the best out of someone, including Gabo. Dahlia was curious to hear what Gabo would say. Maybe the wondrous light had penetrated even Gabo's hard little heart?

"It was probably a curse," Gabo replied.

Dahlia pulled a fresh batch of cookies out of the oven. Her friends were quick to reach for them. Even Simon put up a hand to snag one—without opening his eyes. But Dahlia pulled the tray away from all of them.

"No. This batch is for the king!" she scolded.

Her friends groaned. Simon let his hand fall back to the table with a snore as Dario joined them at the table.

"A squirrel just said good morning to me."

Gabo looked at Dario oddly.

"As squirrels do . . . ?" he replied sarcastically.

"Really? Huh," said Dario, scratching his head. "First for me."

Gabo wasn't alone in giving Dario a strange look. Dario had always marched to the beat of his own drum, but claiming that animals could speak to him was a whole new level of weird.

"Seriously," Gabo whispered to Dahlia, "he wouldn't survive without us."

Dahlia hid a smile but shot Gabo a look to keep him in line.

Suddenly, a loud crash from the nearby chicken room interrupted the friends, and they all turned in the direction of the noise to see Asha, frozen in place. Then, she seemed to almost purposefully knock into a stack of pots piled up next to where she was standing, as if to demonstrate how she had made the noise they had all just heard.

"Ohhh!" Asha exclaimed, rubbing her arm where it had banged into the pots. "I *really* have to watch where I'm going."

Dahlia smiled, relieved to see her friend. Asha was up, dressed and smiling. That had to mean something—even if she was acting a little strange.

"Hey, you touch 'em, you wash 'em," Gabo declared.

He did *not* like having to rewash the pots and pans.

"It was an accident, Gabo," Bazeema chided.

She had materialized next to them at the worktable.

Gabo jumped.

"Where did you—how are you doing that?!"

Bazeema shrugged.

Dahlia still didn't know how Bazeema managed to appear in the kitchens unnoticed, but she didn't have time to think about that now. She needed to focus on Asha.

She hadn't heard what had happened with her interview. Had Asha *not* gotten the job as the king's apprentice? If so, the day before really had been the worst kind of day for Asha, which meant that it was time to do what best friends did best: commiserate, invigorate, and then orchestrate!

Dahlia moved around the others to go to where

Asha was stacking up the pots she had just knocked over.

"Hey, how are you and your poor saba this morning?" she asked quietly.

Dahlia thought back to the day before. They had stood in the same place while they were waiting for Asha to speak with the king. They had been so excited and nervous, so full of hope. A lot had changed in a day.

"Coping . . ." Asha sighed. But then she immediately seemed to snap out of her solemnity.

"And curious," she added quickly with a smile. "How do the kitchens get food up to the king?"

That's an odd response, thought Dahlia. *Why would Asha want to know how the king gets his food? Maybe something about how the food was delivered messed up her interview? Or maybe Asha is feeling touchy about yesterday and wants to change the subject?*

"Oh. Um. The formal servers bring his meals to the dining room," said Dahlia, trying to stay in the moment with Asha.

She was about to say more, about how the servers presented the food, when strange sounds and deep laughter came from the chicken room. Asha let out a loud fake chortle as she looked over her shoulder toward where the strange laughter had come from and then abruptly turned back to Dahlia and leaned in closer.

"So what about when the king eats in his study?" asked Asha, lowering her voice as though she had not just randomly guffawed for no reason. "Who brings it then?"

She was acting very, very strange.

Why was Asha so fixated on this question? Why the study? Maybe she was delirious with disappointment? Dahlia resisted the urge to reach up and feel Asha's forehead to see if she had a fever.

Fine, Dahlia thought. *If Asha doesn't want to talk about how she is feeling after her awful day, I can play along.*

"Well, his study is off-limits," Dahlia explained. Then she paused, cleared her throat, and looked around, motioning for Asha to lean in closer as she lowered her own voice.

"Details are known to only a *select few.*"

She did not explicitly add that she was one of said select few.

But the two friends were too close for Asha not to notice Dahlia's sense of pride for being trusted with such sensitive intel.

"Including you?" asked Asha.

"No comment," said Dahlia, hiding a smile.

Asha gasped excitedly.

It was one of Dahlia's great pleasures working in the kitchen, knowing these kinds of things—like the king's favorite kind of tea on a rainy day, or how he received his food when he was too enthralled in something he was working on up in his study.

In exchange, the utmost loyalty was expected from all those who worked in the castle. It would not be proper—it could even be dangerous—to have such information known widely.

Through the door of the chicken room, Dahlia heard the deep voice again, speaking over muffled squawks and a strange zinging sound.

"Ladies, please. Everyone will get a turn. Form a line. Preferably by height," said the voice's owner.

A man was in the chicken room! And a bright, intense light was flashing out from under the door.

"Who is in there?" Dahlia asked, starting to get a little concerned.

"I don't hear anything," said Asha in a rush, throwing her arm up against the wall to block Dahlia from taking a step toward the chicken room.

Then she leaned forward, speaking urgently in a low voice.

"Dahlia, if you know a secret way into the king's study, you *have* to tell me."

"Why? What is going on with you?" asked Dahlia.

Just then, Safi passed behind them with a sneeze as he walked toward the chicken room.

"Whoa, wait wait wait!" Asha called as she ran after Safi. "What are you doing?"

She leapt in front of the wooden door to the chicken room, blocking his path.

"I gotta collect eggs," said Safi, holding up an empty basket.

Which he does twice a day, Dahlia said to herself. *Which you* know. *Why are you being so strange, Asha?*

"No!" blurted Asha, reaching for Safi's basket. "I mean, let me. I'll do it for you."

"Nah, that's okay, Asha," said Safi, pulling the basket back.

"But your allergies!" Asha exclaimed as she glanced behind her.

Their other friends began to gather around them, curious. Safi always collected the eggs, and Asha had never tried to interfere before.

"Are you trying to take the chickens away from me?" Safi sniffed, with equal parts confusion and sadness.

"You know Safi loves those chickens," Bazeema

added as she placed a hand on Safi's shoulder. She was speaking to Asha as she would have to a small child who needed to be reasoned with.

"I do," agreed Safi, nodding vigorously, clutching his basket.

Everyone knew this was true. Safi treated each chicken with great care and gentleness.

"Are you okay, Asha?" asked Dahlia, wishing that the others would leave. Maybe then she could figure out what was really going on with her friend.

"Something's up with you," said Gabo.

He had reached the same conclusion as Dahlia, though as usual, he couldn't say it with any kindness.

"What are you hiding?" asked Hal, trying to see around Asha.

The teens drew more tightly around Asha.

The noises behind the door grew more intense. Flapping and squawking and the clip-clop of hooves against the stone floor. Hooves? And the occasional chime of something that sounded like music.

"Nothing," Asha replied.

Once again a man's deep voice emanated through the door.

"That's it—life is to be lived!"

"And nobody," Asha added quickly, pressing herself against the door to the chicken room, her arms spread out. She looked desperately at her friends.

"What is going on in there?" Dahlia asked.

Whatever it was, it was certainly having an effect on Asha!

"You look really guilty," said Dario.

It was truly bad when *Dario* thought you were acting strange!

"Friends shouldn't hide things from each other," Hal reminded Asha.

Gabo took a more direct approach.

"Move or we break the door down!" he barked, pointing at the heavy oak door behind Asha.

She put out her hands, palms up, resigned.

"No. No. No. Fine!" she said, rubbing the back of her neck and looking up to the ceiling as if she was trying to find the right words.

The teens quieted down, waiting for an explanation.

"Last night, after everything happened, I made a wish . . ." said Asha, slowly, "on a star. . . ."

"What are you, five?" Gabo interrupted.

Poor Asha, Dahlia thought. *Of course, after Sabino wasn't chosen for the wish granting and Asha didn't get the job as the king's apprentice, wishing on a star kind of made sense.*

Asha must have wanted to do something to find a sense of hope. But what did that have to do with the chicken room and the strange noises coming from behind the door?

"Stop stalling," said Gabo, unsympathetic.

"No! Listen," Asha implored.

She hadn't finished what she had started saying a moment earlier about wishing on a star—before she was so rudely interrupted by Gabo. Once she had everyone's attention, she continued.

"And the star answered."

CHAPTER 9

Asha pushed on the handle and opened the door to the chicken room so her friends could see what was inside.

Their mouths dropped open in shock.

Dahlia threw her right arm out, instinctively feeling the urge to protect her friends behind her from the crazy scene that lay before them. Though she quickly realized nothing about what they beheld could possibly be described as dangerous.

This is real, Dahlia had to remind herself as she took a deep breath. *I am not dreaming. This is real.*

What to take in first? The chickens, singing and dancing together? Or the fact that Asha's pet goat Valentino was *talking*? Talking and . . . *conducting* the chickens in a wildly impressive song and synchronized dance routine?

"That's it, ladies! Your wings can't fly, but your voices can!" Valentino called, tapping his hoof. It was Valentino who spoke in the deep voice Dahlia had heard earlier. (Which was quite surprising coming from a cute baby goat wearing pajamas!)

Dahlia thought back to the day before, when she had told Valentino the story of how she met Asha. It hadn't been a coincidence that he nodded his head at the right moments—he had been listening! He had been trying to communicate with them all along with his bleats; they just couldn't understand him!

But how is he able to talk now? Dahlia was stumped.

"Wow, I have *really* been underestimating animals," said Dario, eyes wide.

Asha seemed to be looking around for something.

Something else? Dahlia wondered. *Something besides this totally crazy musical number performed by chickens and a goat that is happening in front of us?!*

"Amazing, one stick to command them all!" Valentino hollered, waving a feather like a conductor's baton. "Okay, big finish!"

The "big finish" was indeed big and incredibly impressive.

But the *most* surprising part of the finale was the golden-yellow *star* that burst through the cluster of chickens!

The friends let out a collective gasp.

Safi started to sneeze, but everyone held a finger under his nose to stop it. The friends took in the wonder of what was happening. It wasn't just the parts that were unusual—the singing chickens or the talking goat. It was being in the presence of real and true magic. Magic that wanted them to feel loved, to feel all the possibilities of the world.

There is a real living star in front of us! Dahlia wanted to shout. *This is no time for sneezes!*

The star filled the room with a warm, glorious light—it was the very same light that had washed over the kingdom the night before! The star looked happy, which Dahlia had not known was possible for stars. It had a sweet, smiling face and five plump points that extended from its center.

Asha turned to the star.

"These are my friends," she said.

The star floated over to the group of friends to examine each of them. Light as a dandelion puff in a breeze, and sprinkling stardust, it lingered in front of Dahlia.

"Wow. My whole understanding of the natural world is completely turned upside down," she said, basking in the star's wonderful light. "And yet I'm fine with it."

The star gave Dahlia a gentle boop on the nose, then plucked her glasses off her face, tried them on, and accidentally ran into Hal.

"I've never felt so happy in all my life," gushed Hal as the two exchanged smiles. "And that's saying something."

Star—as Asha seemed to call the brilliant ball of light—went to Bazeema next, who waved shyly, giggled, and then ducked behind Hal. This game of peekaboo made Star giggle. Safi came next, though Star's nose-to-nose contact made him sneeze. Star quickly knitted a handkerchief and offered it to Safi.

"Much better than my sleeve," Safi remarked appreciatively. "Thanks!"

Dario was too busy holding a chicken to notice Star heading his way. It appeared that Dario was trying to figure out where, exactly, chickens produced eggs. Star gave Dario a boop on the nose anyway.

"Oh, hey. Thanks!" said Dario casually, then returned to his examination of the chicken as though nothing had happened.

Unlike the others, Simon seemed to confuse

Star. Star studied Simon's face for a few moments, wrinkling its own in concern. Then Star patted Simon's brow in sympathy.

"What? Why do I make you sad?" Simon asked.

Star looked at Asha, who seemed to understand.

"Well . . . Simon's eighteen. He's already given his wish to the king," Asha explained to Star.

"You can feel it?" asked Simon. "I can't remember what I lost."

Star crocheted a tiny heart and pressed it to Simon.

Gabo had been trying to avoid the floating star. He seemed very unnerved and kept ducking behind his friends to hide. Star started following Gabo, as though they were playing a game.

"Ah, stay away. Nope!" Gabo commanded Star.

Then he turned to the others.

"Am I the only one who realizes this is going to end very badly?!"

"Not if everyone keeps quiet about Star," said Asha.

Star peeked around Asha to see Gabo, who ducked away again.

"Magic is forbidden by anyone other than Magnifico," he reminded them. "Our *king*, who is also the only one authorized to grant wishes."

"Self-authorized," Asha clarified.

Star floated over to Simon, leaving a trail of stardust in its wake. Simon rubbed his eyes and took several hard blinks, as though to make sure he wasn't dreaming.

"Does Star grant wishes?" he asked, with a hint of longing in his voice, Dahlia noticed.

"No, but it does seem to want to help me pursue mine," Asha explained.

"Like a fairy godmother," Dario added, as if that were the most normal thing in the world. He was now holding a chicken upside down.

Star had caught up with Gabo again and was

floating in front of his face with a smile. Gabo's eyes went wide with awe, but only for a moment.

"Life is not a fairy tale," Gabo said, partly to Star, partly to himself.

"Depends on how you look at it," Hal countered. "Maybe it could be."

"What did you wish for?" Gabo asked Asha, clearly curious to know more, but then he shook his head. "No, don't tell us. I want no part of this."

His words hung in the air until the sound of trumpets suddenly punctuated the uncomfortable silence.

The *royal* trumpets, sounding from the courtyard.

"That's the king's call to assemble," Bazeema reminded them all.

Everyone turned to look at Asha.

"Please," she begged her friends, holding Star protectively. "Magnifico *can't* know about Star."

Then she lifted her right hand, facing her palm

toward them as though swearing an oath, adding, "And I promise you, my wish won't harm or affect any of you . . . or Rosas."

Star floated up out of Asha's other hand and held up one of its own points, too.

Asha and Dahlia couldn't help giggling at the sight of such a small star making such a big promise.

"That's a big promise, Asha," Simon said, concerned. It was almost as though he had read their minds.

"But we trust you," Hal added quickly, giving Asha a thumbs-up. "Don't we, Bazee— Where did she go?"

Bazeema had vanished again, seemingly right after the king's call but before anyone could notice.

"How does she *do* that?" Gabo screeched.

The trumpets sounded again. It was time to go. And time for them to make their decision. Tell the king, or not?

"It's okay," said Hal. "We won't tell anyone, Asha."

That seemed to make it easier: promising not to tell anyone, rather than promising not to tell the king specifically.

And the king has never said there is a rule we have to tell him things, Dahlia convinced herself.

They weren't doing anything wrong.

"No one would believe me, anyway," Dario mused.

"We got you," said Safi as they all headed out the door for the courtyard, answering the call of their king. He looked at their shortest (and grumpiest) friend. "Right, Gabo?"

Gabo was their weak link. He was the one who'd thought this whole situation was a problem right away. He didn't even really seem to like Star. Gabo folded his arms defiantly.

"I am not happy to be put this position," he said, narrowing his eyes at Asha. "But I don't squeal."

As the others left the room, Dahlia lingered behind. She knew there was something her best friend wasn't telling her.

She needed to speak to Asha.

Alone.

CHAPTER 10

Even with Asha's introducing them to Star and asking that they keep the twinkling friend a secret, Dahlia was sure there was more going on. For starters, they still hadn't talked about what had happened the day before. And then there was that strange, unfinished conversation they had been having where Asha was so curious about how food got to the king.

As soon as the heavy oak door banged shut, Dahlia turned to face her friend and gave her the

"I'm serious" eyes—the ones they only gave each other when they could tell something was up. She placed her right hand on her hip for added impact.

"What are you not telling me?" asked Dahlia urgently, looking into Asha's face.

"Okay, okay," Asha replied. She knew what the "I'm serious" eyes meant, and they didn't have much time to talk—someone might notice they were missing from the assembly in the courtyard.

"Yesterday"—Asha took a deep breath before racing through the rest—"I kind of challenged the king."

It took a moment for the words to sink in.

Asha challenged *the king?*

About what? wondered Dahlia. *How to be the most helpful? Who loved Rosas and its people more?*

"What?" Dahlia asked. She was going to need *a lot* more information.

But in that moment, she flashed back to the wish ceremony the day before, when the king was about to bestow Sania's wish. What had he said?

I have been challenged today to take a chance and try something new.

Asha hung her head.

"It's, uh, complicated," she said, clasping her hands in front of her. She sounded kind of . . . pained.

"And . . . ?" Dahlia continued.

Unlike some of the others, Dahlia knew that sometimes more talking did not make a person talk more. It might even make them quieter. So she waited for Asha, holding her gaze and letting the silence grow larger and larger.

Finally, Asha broke it.

"Dahlia," said Asha, looking at her friend earnestly with her big brown eyes. "What would you do if you found out the wishes of those you love with all your heart will never be granted?"

She was almost pleading with Dahlia. And she was fiddling with her coral necklace, a surefire sign that she was anxious about something.

"You mean your saba's wish?" asked Dahlia

softly, trying to calm her best friend, but also clarify Asha's meaning.

"And, thanks to me, my mother's," Asha added sadly, letting out a sigh. "I'm here to get their wishes so I can give them back to them," she explained.

Dahlia felt dizzy. She must have been misunderstanding what Asha was saying.

"You're here to *steal* from the king?" She gaped, hoping the answer was no.

At that, Star suddenly zoomed up to Asha's side, shaking its entire body as if saying *no no no!*

"It's not stealing," insisted Asha, sounding more resolved than worried. "The wishes *don't* belong to him."

"And you . . . can't just ask Magnifico for them back?" asked Dahlia.

That was what they were supposed to do—ask for what they wanted from the king.

"I think I've ruined my chances of asking Magnifico for anything," Asha replied soberly.

Dahlia saw the pain in her best friend's eyes.

Even still, what if Asha was wrong? What if Dahlia helped Asha take back her family's wishes, and the king found out and became furious? He might refuse *her* wish, or her family's wishes, when the time came. Or say that she could no longer be the castle baker!

But Dahlia knew Asha, and she knew that she needed to trust her, like she always did. And with good reason, too. Asha had never led Dahlia astray. She had never done anything to hurt her or get her into trouble. In fact, Dahlia saw time and time again how Asha went out of her way to help those around her.

The trumpets sounded again. Dahlia had to do something.

Maybe, just this once, it would be okay to break the rules. In fact, it wasn't really even *breaking* them. Just bending them a little. Like how she shaped warm melted sugar into something beautiful to place on top of a cake—she always knew when to stop pushing the sugar; too far and it would crack.

Dahlia could be flexible, too.

She could do this.

Dahlia nodded and led Asha, Star, and Valentino out of the chicken room and over to what looked like a wooden cabinet door. She pulled a key from her apron pocket. When she unlocked the door and opened it, she revealed a dumbwaiter—a large box that could be raised and lowered on pulleys between the different levels of the castle.

"This is how we get food to the king's study," Dahlia explained, giving the rope a tug.

When the food in the dumbwaiter reached the king, he could simply open the door in his office and take out the food without anyone disturbing him.

Asha and Star peered in, astonished.

Then Asha hugged Dahlia.

"It's *perfect*," she gushed.

Without another word, Asha squeezed herself into the dumbwaiter. Star floated in next to her.

"A new way to climb!" Valentino called as he leapt in, too, and turned around.

"Backing up," he warned.

Clearly, Valentino was not going to let Asha go without him.

"Okay, look out!" Asha grunted from inside. "We can't fit. Oh. Ugh."

Dahlia started having second thoughts. This was not a good idea. She served at the pleasure of the king, and now she was helping her best friend—and her best friend's talking goat and magical star!—sneak into his study by showing them the dumbwaiter, a secret known only to select castle staff. They were all going to get into trouble.

Huge trouble.

A literal ton of trouble.

Maybe I can still talk Asha out of this plan, she thought.

"Are you sure about this?" Dahlia asked through gritted teeth as she looked around. "Magnifico could come back at any time."

Just the thought of Magnifico finding Asha in his study made Dahlia blanch.

Her idea to convince Asha quickly backfired.

"And that's why you're going to stall him. Please and thank you, best friend ever?" Asha begged in a rush with an imploring look on her face.

"How am I supposed to stall a king?!" Dahlia asked, flabbergasted.

She did *not* like making things up. That was why she was a baker. Baking told you exactly what to do and how to do it. If you skipped a step or didn't measure the ingredients precisely, you usually ended up with a disaster. But if you followed the instructions perfectly, you got a beautiful cake or pie.

"You'll think of something," said Asha confidently as she shut the door to the dumbwaiter.

"You're a genius!" she added, her voice muffled by the wooden barrier between them.

Then she must have turned to Valentino, because Dahlia heard their conversation.

"Oh, to the left," Asha instructed.

"Let's go up!" Valentino said, excitedly.

"I have to reach the pulley thing," Asha explained.

"And we ride!" the goat cheered. Then Dahlia heard him apologize to Asha. "I'm sorry, that was right in your ear."

The dumbwaiter started to inch its way upward. Dahlia could tell from the squeaking sounds of the pulley within.

Asha's and Valentino's voices grew fainter and fainter until Dahlia could only imagine what they were saying to each other.

She dreaded carrying out the promise she had made to her best friend, but she couldn't wait any longer. It was time to go out into the courtyard and join the others. She had to save any stalling for the king!

As she headed outside, Dahlia hoped the king would be in a particularly loquacious mood. Maybe she wouldn't have to say a word to him? Maybe he'd be so chatty he'd stall himself?

But that was just wishful thinking. . . .

CHAPTER 11

The energy of the crowd that had gathered in the courtyard upon the king's call was divided between excitement and curiosity. The audience hummed with anticipation.

Why was the king assembling them for a second day in a row?

Maybe it was another wish-granting ceremony!

As she made her way through the throngs of townsfolk to find her friends, Dahlia also heard a fair amount of chatter about the mysterious light from the night before—*Star's light,* which was no longer a mystery to her and her friends. She tried to make her face as neutral as possible as she passed, but snippets of lively conversations about the lovely glow that had fallen over the kingdom floated around her.

"—can't believe that light last night."

"That light was amazing!"

"—like nothing I've ever seen . . ."

When Dahlia finally found her group, they looked at one other, trying not to say too much or too little. Too much, and they might spill the secret about Star. Too little, and they might look like they were hiding something.

King Magnifico and Queen Amaya appeared on the steps before them, looking as regal and elegant as always. The king put out his hands, hushing the crowd.

"Quiet, quiet, quiet!" the king commanded.

Does his voice sound more brusque than usual? Dahlia wondered.

She had spent so much time swooning over

his different tones, she knew them more than she would have liked to admit.

Magnifico continued.

"I know you are all wondering about that little light last night."

The crowd began to cheer, clearly thinking that the king was going to say that the light was a gift he had bestowed upon them. But King Magnifico frowned with annoyance.

"A light I did not command or condone!" he bellowed.

Dahlia flinched. The king's words stung like a cinder from one of the kitchens' blazing ovens.

The townsfolk's cheers turned into murmured questions, and rumbles of confusion burbled up from the crowd.

"It *was* magic," Magnifico clarified. "Though quite clumsy and amateurish. It was also completely forbidden!"

When the king said *forbidden*, Dahlia felt sick. What was happening?

"There is a traitor amongst us who defied the law!" The king was now impassioned as he spoke. "They used magic to put you all at risk!"

Dahlia had never heard the king speak in such a way. It was as if he was trying to scare them all. What law was he talking about? And by *traitor*, did he mean Asha? Asha hadn't meant to summon Star—it had just . . . happened. And Dahlia couldn't believe that Star would harm any of them!

The rest of Rosas didn't know that, though, and a growing wave of shock and fear began to churn through the crowd. Dahlia watched it happen, confused and alarmed. To her, it seemed as though King Magnifico was whipping up the crowd with his words the same way she might whip egg whites into a meringue.

"But don't worry," he then promised, in a voice that was strong and steady. "They are no match for me, and I assure you: when caught, they will be punished severely."

Punished.

Severely.

Dahlia's friends exchanged guilty looks. They didn't even know what Asha was up to inside the castle at that very moment, or that Dahlia had helped her. She looked up at the windows toward the king's study, biting her lower lip with concern. She hoped that Asha was okay, and that she was moving quickly.

"I ask you to keep your eyes and ears open," said the king. "Any information will be most helpful. Rosas needs you."

With a sweep of his cape, the king turned to go.

"And I know you will never, ever let me down," he added. "Thank you."

Dahlia's stomach churned.

Now the king was making it clear he expected them to tell him about Asha. And Star. Dahlia was definitely breaking the rules. She was letting her king down. He had just said so! And what was more, he was going back inside, where Asha, Valentino, and Star were. Asha had asked her to stall him, but what was she supposed to do? Dahlia swallowed and tried to think. She just needed more time to come up with an idea.

"Your Majesty, wait! Please!"

The words left her mouth before she had even thought them through, and they seemed to part the crowd like a spoon swiped through freshly whipped cream. The king was looking straight at Dahlia—and so was everyone else. Hundreds of eyes fell on her, but the brilliant blue of the king's seemed to lock onto hers, and she couldn't look away.

"Yes, go on," the king answered.

He seemed weary and impatient. Not at all the usual good-natured leader that Dahlia had had a crush on since that fateful day all those years before when she'd received his invitation to visit the castle to bake.

Dahlia cleared her throat, trying to think of

something intelligent to say. Maybe she should introduce herself?

"Hi, I'm Dahlia," she said.

That was a good start. But then she looked in his eyes again and lost her train of thought.

"Goodness, your eyes are that sparkly, objectively."

She couldn't believe she had just said that to him. Out loud! She cringed to herself, although she thought maybe the compliment would help change his mood.

"What can I do for you, Dahlia?" groaned the king, who did not sound like he wanted to do anything for her at the moment.

Dahlia racked her brain.

"Thank you for asking," she stalled. "You said any information would be helpful."

She was just repeating what he'd said. What kind of question could she muster? *Think, Dahlia!*

"But pragmatically speaking, what qualifies?" she asked.

Oh, that sounded like something!

Dahlia continued. "Evidentiary? How about circumstantial? Firsthand, secondhand, well, then there's third . . ."

There, she had come up with a question. Technically *three* questions. Three terrible questions, plus some extra rambling, but they would have to do.

Luckily, someone else in the crowd picked up on the idea.

"How about hunches?" someone called out.

Dahlia's questions had gotten the crowd in a more inquisitive mood. She couldn't believe it! Her horrible attempt at stalling had miraculously worked!

"Thank you," said Dahlia eagerly. "Though I doubt it—how about hunches?"

"Yes, ANY," Magnifico replied with impatience. "ANY information about who or what caused the light would be helpful. So, yes, hunch. Hunch away."

"You said it was amateur magic," another person chimed in. "But how come you don't know how they did it?"

The crowd murmured in agreement.

Didn't the king know everything about magic?

"What?" spat Magnifico. He had clearly taken the question as an insult, a slight against his own magical abilities.

No, no, no! Dahlia thought. *This is not what was supposed to happen! Just a few minutes to stall, that was all Asha asked for! Now the situation is getting out of hand.*

"Perhaps you could define 'amateur,'" Dahlia prompted, trying to smooth things over and take the lead again.

This is what happens when things get messy, Dahlia's inner baker reminded her. *When rules aren't followed, things get out of control.*

"This is about what *you* know," Magnifico haughtily reminded the crowd. "It is about your safety and, most importantly, the safety of your wishes."

If the king thought his comment would settle the crowd, he was mistaken.

"Wait. You mean our wishes aren't safe?" another person asked.

It was a voice near Dahlia. She looked around to see that it was Simon who had asked that one. She shot him a sharp look as the crowd erupted into worried murmurs.

Maybe their king was not as powerful as they had thought. . . .

Dahlia tried to turn things around.

"Of course they're safe!" she insisted, gritting her teeth.

She was literally lying *through* her teeth, and the lie was as heavy as the earthen pots that lined the walls of the castle kitchens. At that very moment, Asha was trying to take back two of the wishes! Sure, they belonged to her own family members, but still! If Asha could sneak in and retrieve wishes, didn't that mean that someone else could, too—someone whose intentions were perhaps less pure?

Dahlia couldn't shake the bitter taste all of this left in her mouth.

The king was acting so very odd, too. Maybe he was more worried about the light Star had washed over the kingdom than he let on. But Star was so sweet.

Perhaps this is all a misunderstanding!

The hopeful thought dawned on Dahlia. But as she struggled to figure out what to do next, the crowd grew more restless and started calling out all kinds of questions.

"How do we know our wishes are safe?" a woman in the crowd asked. "We never see them!"

"Yes, why can't we see them? Why is that a rule?"

"And why can't we remember them?"

"One question at a time," Dahlia called, trying to regain control.

"Since we're asking," interrupted another person. "What about if we want to change our wish?"

"Good point, wishes can change," said someone else.

"Let's form a line. Everyone will get a turn," Dahlia instructed.

"You know what would comfort us all the most?" another person in the crowd proposed. "Another wish ceremony."

That suggestion energized the townsfolk even more.

"Great idea!"

"We could do it now!"

"It would make us all feel so much better."

"A wish ceremony!

"Please, Your Majesty!"

"We could do it now!"

"No!" Dahlia shouted. "Not now! Bad timing!"

She could see the king growing more and more annoyed. No, not annoyed—angry. The king was angry.

The crowd kept at it.

"Oh, please!

"Please! Please!"

"Please, Your Majesty!"

"Oh, please, Your Majesty!"

The voices were joining together, becoming a single plea. They wanted a wish. They felt someone should get a wish.

"Silence!" ordered King Magnifico. "Is that all you can think about? A wish-granting ceremony?"

Dahlia's thoughts swirled. She was supposed to be stalling the king. To protect Asha *from* the king—who was supposed to be the person who protected all of them! But if he was their protector, why was he so angry with his people? He seemed disgusted with them, but the crowd wasn't catching on. Their faces all shone upward toward him; they were so eager for him to grant the wishes that they had entrusted to him, the wishes that he had promised he would grant when the time was right.

"Fine," the king answered, pointing at the people gathered before him. "Whoever identifies the traitor, your wish will be granted!"

The crowd went wild.

Dahlia felt her insides squeeze together. Now everyone would be on the lookout. With vigor. How would Asha be able to keep Star a secret now?

Simon leaned over to Dahlia.

"Offering to grant another wish? He must really be worried."

"But hear this!" the king added, fixing them all with a stern stare. "Anyone who helps the traitor, anyone who lets me down, your wish will *never* be granted."

Dahlia and her friends all looked at one another, worried.

"Might I suggest," Gabo hissed, "you all try not to look so guilty."

Dario wiggled his ears.

Dahlia looked back at the king. He had never done anything to shake her trust, but Asha had said that he was withholding her family's wishes to punish her. And now he was threatening the whole kingdom that he would do the same to them.

Was it right to separate someone from their most heartfelt wish?

King Magnifico began to march back into the castle, still fuming.

"Wait! Your Majesty!" Dahlia called after him.

She didn't know if Asha had succeeded in her plan. They hadn't even agreed on a sign so that Dahlia could know that Asha had left the king's study and was safe.

"Please, what qualifies as letting you down?" Dahlia yelled, her last—failed—attempt to get the king to turn around.

It didn't matter.

The roar of the crowd drowned out Dahlia's voice.

CHAPTER 12

"Busy hands soothe a worried heart."

That was what Dahlia's grandmother had said when times were rough. Instead of sitting and stewing, Dahlia's grandmother taught her to get up, move around. Sweep the floor. Weed the garden. Make the bed. Take a walk.

Bake a cake.

Dahlia was feeling so anxious after the king's assembly that she knew baking one cake wouldn't do the trick. So she decided to bake two treats— the jidangao for Simon (again!) and some orange cranberry scones for the king's breakfast the next morning.

She set about gathering all her ingredients for both recipes, placing each item in its own separate dish and setting them out on the worktable in two little groupings, allowing her mind to settle with the order of what lay before her.

Preparing and setting out ingredients always made Dahlia feel more in control. Everything had a place and was neatly organized. The flour went in the large blue bowls, the sugar in the smaller red ones. The eggs had already been cracked open, the bright yellow yolks floating in green bowls like small suns over verdant little pastures.

Ingredients with smaller quantities were lined up in petite white dishes—salt, orange zest, cranberries she had dried in the sun. Dahlia retrieved a weighty rectangle of butter from one crock and poured out a cup of buttermilk from another. The thick ceramic walls of the crocks kept the dairy products cool and unspoiled. Then she pressed a few oranges, pouring their sweet, pulpy juice into a small white pitcher.

When Dahlia had finished her prep work, the worktable was full, but orderly. To her left, all the ingredients for the jidangao seemed to smile up at her hopefully, while the gaggle of items she'd need for the scones waited patiently on her right.

Bazeema suddenly appeared next to the baking station.

"Stress baking, huh?"

Dahlia nearly dropped the bowl of eggs.

"Bazeema!"

It was just the two of them in the kitchen, not the usual hum of helpers coming and going. She should have been able to hear Bazeema enter; at least, she probably could have heard her if she had not been so wrapped up in her own thoughts.

"Where did you come from?" she asked.

Bazeema smiled timidly.

"The place where I was," her bashful friend

answered mysteriously as she peered at the countertop covered in bowls and crocks.

"Two recipes going at once! You really are stressed."

"I have to do something," said Dahlia fretfully. "I can't just sit around while I wait for news."

She didn't dare say Asha's name, but Bazeema caught her meaning.

"I haven't heard anything, either," she said quietly. Bazeema gestured toward the worktable. "What are you making?"

"I'm trying to make jidangao again," said Dahlia. "For Simon. Maybe the fourth time's the charm? And orange cranberry scones for the king's breakfast."

Dahlia did not add that she knew the scones usually put the king in a good mood, which he seemed to need, desperately.

"I've been working on a new design," Bazeema told her.

Bazeema braided different-colored thread into beautiful and intricately patterned bracelets, belts, bookmarks, and beyond.

"Weaving and thinking," she added. "Can I watch you bake?"

"Of course," said Dahlia, smiling. "The company would be nice."

Dahlia started with the jidangao, beating the eggs until her arm ached and then adding sugar in batches. Her grandmother told her that the batter was ready for flour when she could write the number 8 in the batter without it disappearing.

"Can you put a pan of water on the stove?" Dahlia asked Bazeema. "This cake is steamed, not baked."

Bazeema nodded, setting down her thread and fetching a pan as Dahlia moved to add the next few ingredients.

It was nice having Bazeema there with her. Asha, too, was always happy to find pans or missing ingredients for Dahlia whenever she stopped by the kitchens for a visit.

Asha.

Dahlia had not seen her friend since she had crawled inside the dumbwaiter and shut the door. But there was no one she could tell her worries to—that would just make it more likely that Asha would be found and punished as a traitor. She hoped Asha was safe. She hoped that, somehow, everything would be okay.

"Would this one work?" Bazeema asked, interrupting Dahlia's worries, holding up a flat copper pan.

"Oh, uh, the bigger one is better," said Dahlia, distractedly. She tilted her head in the direction of a larger pan on the shelf as she added another ingredient to the cake batter.

"Just like that one, but bigger."

Bazeema swapped out the pan for the larger one while Dahlia poured the batter into four smaller pans, arranged them in the steamer, and put it on the large copper pan.

"If I do it right, the top will crack and look like a smiling face," she explained to Bazeema.

"How do you know so much about everything?" Bazeema asked.

"My grandma," Dahlia answered with a sigh, smiling to herself as she remembered her grandmother sharing that same baking tip with her years before.

"She taught me so much, and not just about baking. She was also a healer—did you know that you can use honey to cure a wound?"

Bazeema shook her head.

"Whenever I got burned by the oven, my grandmother would put a little honey on the spot to help it heal. It always seemed to work, so I make sure to keep some on hand. Good thing Hal keeps us freshly stocked," Dahlia added with a wink as she moved on to start making the scones.

She mixed the dry ingredients together and cut in the butter. Dahlia always enjoyed this process of incorporating butter by slicing it with a special tool that allowed her to mix it into the dry ingredients—watching the pieces become smaller and smaller until the mixture looked like sand—without the warmth of her hands melting the butter into a paste. The small bits of butter, now scattered evenly throughout the scone mixture, needed to stay as chilled as possible so that once inside the oven they'd melt, leaving airy pockets of buttery goodness in each delicious bite.

"Now for the wet ingredients," announced Dahlia.

She was feeling calmer. This was her space, the place where she felt the happiest and the safest.

"Buttermilk, lemon zest, orange ju—" She stopped, her hand grabbing for something that wasn't there.

"What's the matter?" asked Bazeema.

"The orange juice. It was right there," said Dahlia, pointing at the spot where the orange juice was supposed to be.

"In a small white pitcher?" asked Bazeema.

"Yessss?"

"Like that one?"

Now Bazeema was pointing to the side of the worktable where Dahlia had been making the jidangao. The small pitcher stood empty next to where the bowl of cake batter had been.

"What? No! Oh no!" Dahlia felt like crying. "I added the orange juice to the wrong batter?! That's not supposed to happen!"

She replayed the last hour in her mind. Maybe when she was worrying about Asha she had gotten distracted? Or when she was helping Bazeema pick the right-sized pan? Or when she was talking about her grandmother? Maybe she had put the orange juice with the wrong set of ingredients from the start? It didn't matter. However she had done it, there was no way to get the orange juice out of the cake.

Bazeema put her arm around Dahlia.

"It's okay. You have more oranges for the scones, right?"

Dahlia took her glasses off and rubbed the spot where they perched on her nose.

"That's not the part I'm upset about," Dahlia said with a sigh. "I'm not supposed to put orange juice in the jidangao. It's all wrong now."

Bazeema sniffed the air.

"It doesn't *smell* bad," she said cautiously.

"It's not in the recipe," Dahlia moaned miserably. "I can't make it perfectly even when I try following the recipe to the letter—can you imagine what will happen now that I've added a whole new ingredient?"

She reached to take the steamer off the stove. There was no point in letting the cake finish. But Bazeema stopped her.

"You've come this far," Bazeema offered. "You might as well see what happens."

"It will be a disaster," predicted Dahlia. "A complete and utter disaster."

Bazeema cocked her head to one side and smiled gently. That was her way of saying, *Really?*

Maybe she had a point.

"Okay. We might as well let it finish steaming," Dahlia said, relenting. "Then we can see how much of a mess it will be."

If I gave the king my wish, and he granted it, this would never happen! she told herself. *Everything would always turn out perfectly.*

That was a good enough reason to give her wish to the king. Or it would be, once everything with Asha and Star was ironed out. . . .

⋆⋅✦⁺⁺⋆

Dahlia didn't want to face the ruined jidangao, so she took her time. She removed them from the steamer when she was supposed to in order to let them cool a bit, and then tested the scones before she took them out of the oven—giving the pan a turn to check each of them for the exact shade of golden brown she had memorized that she knew meant they were finished.

"Now?" Bazeema asked shyly, holding up the steamed cakes. She didn't seem nearly as concerned about Dahlia's baking snafu of epic proportions.

At least they have split properly on top, Dahlia noticed.

"Let's wait until I finish cleaning," she grumbled, to delay her inevitable disappointment just a little longer.

Dahlia washed the bowls and utensils, making sure each item was thoroughly clean. She wiped down the worktables and the counters and put away all the ingredients. She put the orange rinds in a bin to give to the pigs in their pen later and swept the floor.

"Better get 'em while they're still warm!" Bazeema smile encouragingly and gestured toward the cakes. "They smell really good!"

Dahlia tried not to sigh. Bazeema was just trying to be a good friend, and if the situation were reversed, Dahlia would do the same thing—encouraging her, trying to make the best of it. It was just . . . there was no chance the cakes had turned out. Oranges did not belong in the recipe. It was as simple as that. They wouldn't have the *gu zao wei*—the old-style aroma—from the eggs. She still could not believe she had done something so foolish.

Bazeema took the first bite and dropped her fork, and her eyes widened in surprise.

"You can spit it out!" cried Dahlia, alarmed. "Just spit it out!"

Poor Bazeema! She was probably forcing herself to swallow the horrible-tasting cake just to spare Dahlia's feelings.

"See?! I told you it would be terrible!"

Bazeema swallowed and smiled.

"Actually, it's delicious."

She took another, larger bite to prove her point.

What?

Dahlia took a tiny, cautious bite. Her taste buds suddenly felt like they were filled with sunlight. Happiness. An orange cloud.

"It's good!" she said, astonished.

She took another bite just to make sure it wasn't a fluke. It was actually more than good—it was delicious! It might not have tasted like her grandmother's cake, but it made her *feel* the way she had felt baking beside her grandmother all those years before: excited, curious, giddy! It was light and pillowy and pleasingly sweet. She had never had anything like it.

"This isn't possible," she murmured, studying the cake. "This wasn't . . ."

"In the recipe?" Bazeema finished for her.

"Exactly," said Dahlia. "I mean, I thought my grandmother had perfected this recipe."

"Maybe she had made the perfect recipe for *her*, but not for *you*," Bazeema suggested after she swallowed another bite. "Don't get me wrong. The other recipe was really good, too. But maybe making what you're really craving means not following the recipe sometimes?"

Dahlia pondered Bazeema's words.

"It was partly luck, though," said Dahlia. "What if I had been making, I don't know, a carrot cake? I don't think carrots would have worked!"

She gestured toward the cake, pretending that several whole carrots were sticking out.

"Oh! And some stalks of celery," Bazeema said with a smile, playing along.

"And one whole onion," said Dahlia, pantomiming a whole onion falling into the cake.

They burst into giggles. Oh, it felt good to

laugh. After the stress of the day—worrying about Asha, feeling their king's disapproval—being silly was just the antidote!

"Then don't do that the next time!" Bazeema suggested, yanking the pretend vegetables out of the cake.

"I can make a whole new mistake then!" said Dahlia, laughing even harder. "Maybe I'll add . . . butaragas!"

Bazeema raised an eyebrow. "What?"

"The vegetable! You know. Rubagatas!"

The word Dahlia was trying for was *rutabaga*. But the harder she tried, the more the word seemed to elude her.

"Do you mean rutababas?" Bazeema asked. "No! I mean—"

Dahlia interrupted. "Rutagabas!"

The whole effort sent the two friends into a gale of laughter and giggles. They gave up trying to say the right word. They were overcome by the kind of laughter that, when they started to wind down, one of them only had to say some version of *rutabaga* to start them laughing all over again.

Then they started speaking in rutabaga.

"Cake-abaga," said Bazeema in their nonsense language as she held up another cake.

"Too-good-abaga!" agreed Dahlia, emphatically taking a bite.

This sent them into another fit of laughter.

Finally, after many more rounds of giggles, they calmed down.

"If your mistakes sometimes taste like this," proposed Bazeema, helping herself to the last cake, "I think it's worth it."

"Fair enough," said Dahlia, smiling.

Then she thought about Asha again.

Had she made a mistake helping Asha get her family's wishes back? If so, she really hoped the whole situation would somehow turn out as well as her new orange-infused jidangao.

CHAPTER 13

As the afternoon wore on, everything seemed almost . . . *fine*. Dahlia thought about laughing in the kitchen with Bazeema and about the amazing new cake she had made imperfectly perfect, totally on accident, and she smiled.

But she still worried about Asha. How could she not? She hadn't heard from her friend in hours. That was rare even when nothing was going on, but when a magical star had fallen from the sky and their handsome sorcerer-king was angrily obsessed with it and whoever had brought it down to their kingdom, the lack of communication felt *especially* wrong.

Where was she? Was she okay? Maybe Asha would pop her head into the kitchens at any moment, and they could pretend everything was normal. Perhaps this whole thing about Star would calm down. The king would see Star was no big deal. Maybe no one would notice Asha's family's missing wishes—or! Or maybe Asha had not been successful and hadn't taken either Sabino's or Sakina's wishes at all.

But the air in Rosas did not feel right. Dahlia could sense something was off as she stepped out of the castle to take her kitchen scraps to the pigs in their pen. Perhaps it was her nose for baking, sensing differences in the unseen. The air felt thick and electric, like the moments before a storm.

Then she saw them: pieces of parchment hanging all around the kingdom. They had been freshly painted with images of Asha and Star, and they were posted everywhere! People gathered around them and spoke in suspicious whispers full of confusion and anger. Dahlia could not hear exactly what they were saying, but she knew none of it was good.

"Asha! I don't believe it—"

"—stealing and destroying wishes?"

Dahlia's stomach churned. What was happening? Asha—wanted as a traitor to the king? It made no sense. Asha—who was so kind and sweet and helpful? How could they believe she was an enemy? And all because of Star?

The whole world seemed to have turned upside down.

A trumpet sounded. Another assembly. Dahlia left her scraps with the pigs and made her way to the wish-granting arena, where she found a few of her friends—Safi, Hal, Dario, and Gabo—huddled together. Dahlia wondered where Simon and Bazeema were, and Asha. Where was Asha?

On the stage, a guard stood over three silent,

grief-stricken people holding one another's hands as they sat together. It was as though they were on display for the whole kingdom to see.

"Look at these poor people!" the guard called out to the crowd. "Asha stole and destroyed their wishes! She must pay!"

The crowd buzzed with shock and concern.

"Asha?"

"Is it true?"

"I can't believe it."

"She seemed so sweet."

Dahlia and her friends were just as bewildered.

"They say her family's gone missing," said Safi, wide-eyed.

Dahlia gasped.

Not Saba and Sakina! She hoped they were safe. Where could they have gone? But more than anything, she hoped *Asha* was safe. She could almost swear that her best-friend senses were tingling; could Asha be close by? No. She wouldn't have come to—what seemed to Dahlia, at least—the epicenter of the king's witch hunt against her. It was too dangerous. No, she wouldn't have.

Would she?

Dahlia glanced around, just to be sure. But there were too many people milling about. So many different cloaks and headscarves, it was impossible to make out each and every face.

"Boy, you think you know somebody," said Gabo, distracting Dahlia from her search.

None of what was going on in Rosas made any sense anymore, and she found herself feeling suspicious of everything.

"This whole thing feels wrong," Dahlia declared.

Suddenly, green magic shot out across the stage!

This was different from anything the king had created before.

The audience screamed and cowered as the

ominous light contorted and pulsed over them, zooming over their heads and making aggressive swoops at the crowd. People gasped and cried out as they ducked in fear.

For a moment, the green magic over the crowd formed what looked like huge hands, ready to grab them.

Then, laughter—of all things—interrupted their frightened screams.

It was Magnifico, swaggering onto to the stage. He was holding a long silvery staff with an ornate mirror at the top. Dahlia had never seen the king with it before. With a snap of the king's hand, the oppressive magic dissipated. The crowd looked to the king, trying to reconcile their terror with the king's apparent joy. If he cared that he had frightened his people, he did not show it.

"Ha! Your faces!" Magnifico bellowed. "It's okay. You're okay. It's just a play on light."

The crowd clapped and cheered, so eager to believe him.

The king smiled, but it wasn't his usual comforting, handsome smile. This one seemed sharper, a little mean. He twirled the staff.

"You know I love you, Rosas."

Why is he treating us this way? thought Dahlia.

He was being a bully, tricking them by switching between cruelty and kindness.

Behind the king, Queen Amaya took slow, careful steps out onto the stage, her head bowed. She sat next to the people whose wishes had been crushed, reaching out to take one of their hands and holding it gently in hers.

Queen Amaya feels closer to those people hurting onstage than she does to the king, Dahlia realized.

And now Dahlia was questioning everything she herself had believed about Magnifico. She had always thought he was perfect, inside and out. He was so incredibly handsome, and he had bestowed the people of Rosas with their wishes, and kept them safe, and given them everything they could want . . . or so she thought. He wouldn't give

Asha what she wanted, or Sabino or Sakina, and why was that? Because Asha had challenged him? Wouldn't a good king not be frightened by some honest questions? Didn't fair rulers want more than blind followers?

Maybe she had been wrong all along about Magnifico.

"You are probably wondering why you're all here," said the king, framed by a spotlight onstage.

Some people in the crowd turned and looked at the pieces of parchment hanging throughout the kingdom. The reason seemed obvious.

"Yes, there's a savage teenager running around with a star destroying wishes," Magnifico explained dismissively.

Even when he said the words, the king did not sound like he believed them to be true. His face broke out in a huge smile.

"BUT . . . guess who bravely came forward and identified her?"

In a brief second, Dahlia realized it must have

been someone in their group. Who else cou
have known about Star?

But who was it? Not Bazeema, wherever sh
was. And it couldn't have been Hal or Safi. Gabo?
She glanced over to see if Gabo's expression had
changed. Did he look happy? Gabo claimed he
was no snitch, but . . .

CHAPTER 14

The curtains behind the king opened, revealing Simon standing awkwardly onstage.

"Give a big cheer for SIMON O'DONOHUE!" roared King Magnifico.

The friends all gasped in horror.

No! Dahlia's heart felt like it might stop beating. *Not Simon. Not sleepy, sweet Simon. Wasn't he just encouraging Asha before her interview?*

But there he was, smiling nervously as the astonished crowd clapped for him. Dahlia and her friends exchanged bewildered looks, but no one dared say a thing. One wrong word could get the rest of them in trouble.

Simon took a few tentative steps toward Magnifico.

"I know! I know!" said the king in a jolly tone. "I was just as surprised as you all. Our sleepy little Simon here. No need to be nervous, Simon."

The king clapped a hand on the teen's broad shoulder and gestured toward the people out in the crowd.

"Be proud!" urged the king. "Show us your joy!"

The king, Dahlia now understood, could be nice when he wanted to be. When it served him to be nice.

"Yay, Rosas," said Simon weakly, still hunched over.

His voice could barely be heard over the cheers of the crowd. Dahlia felt frozen in place. First Asha was labeled a traitor to the king and an enemy of Rosas, and now Simon had betrayed Asha. What could happen next?

Why did you do it, Simon? Dahlia wondered. *What could possibly be worth it?*

"So, my dear Simon," the king continued. "Are you ready to see your wish?"

That was why Simon had betrayed Asha. For his wish.

He held up Simon's wish for everyone to see.

"TO BE THE KING'S MOST VALIANT, COURAGEOUS, AND LOYAL KNIGHT!"

Simon stared at his wish for a moment, not moving. He still seemed half-awake, even as the air was filled with roars of approval and applause. All for Simon.

The king said his wish was to be loyal?

"Just not a loyal *friend*," Gabo spat.

"Such betrayal," said Bazeema, appearing next to Gabo suddenly.

Gabo whirled around.

"Bazeema, we were worried about you," he whispered.

The friends turned their attention back to the

stage. The king had begun swirling his magic around Simon, waving his new staff in large, dramatic arcs. Simon rose in the air as if pulled by an invisible string.

King Magnifico lifted his arms.

"It is my great pleasure to grant you your heart's desire," he thundered.

Dahlia had seen dozens of wish grantings in her lifetime. It was supposed to be a moment of great joy, the essence of the wish coming true. But this time things were different. The magic surrounding Simon was green and sinister—the same shade of green light that had transformed into the crushing hands—and then, like a boa constrictor, it began coiling around and squeezing Simon. It was crushing him! Simon let out a terrible cry of pain, a howl that Dahlia felt in her bones.

Stop! she wanted to cry out. *You're hurting him!*

Suddenly, panels of intimidating armor began affixing themselves to Simon, covering him bit by bit until he was completely encased. He landed on the stage with a thud, his arms raised, his feet planted apart. A fighting stance. A large sword flashed in his hand.

"Long live the king!" bellowed Simon in a strangely emphatic voice Dahlia did not recognize. Simon stood up straight and bowed to the king.

Bazeema put her hand on Dahlia's shoulder.

"We need to go. *Now*."

Dahlia could see that the others already stood at the edge of the crowd, waiting to go.

From the stage, Magnifico smiled approvingly.

"Isn't that wonderful. Tell us, Simon—"

Dahlia was not looking anymore. She was too busy following the others as Dario helped her make her way through the crowd, dodging people, bumping against moss-studded stone walls. Time seemed to slow. It might have been only seconds that passed, but it felt like an eternity. Dahlia tried to focus on the sound of her crutch against the ground below to take her mind off what she sensed was coming any moment. With each reliable tap against the stones, she knew she was getting closer toward wherever it was Bazeema was leading them, and she trusted Bazeema instinctively, even if her friend did seemingly appear and disappear out of thin air at odd moments.

Then she heard it, the something else she had been dreading. The new Simon—was he even really the Simon she had known?—had not even waited for Magnifico to finish his sentence before he proved himself to be the king's most loyal knight.

"There are six more traitors in the crowd, sir," Simon interjected in a monotone voice.

Dahlia gasped. Her friend's betrayal was complete. She almost stopped walking, but Hal urged her to keep going.

Dahlia heard a loud clang: the sound of a sword being slammed onto the stage.

"Irresponsible teens," Simon barked.

There was none of the usual warmth in his voice, no caring. He said their names with disgust.

"Dahlia, Gabo, Dario, Safi, Hal, and Bazeema."

"This way," instructed Bazeema in a hushed voice.

From the stage, Magnifico's voice boomed.

"Find them so they may pay for their betrayal. Find Asha so you may be rewarded. But most importantly, find me that star so I will have the power to grant all of your wishes!"

The crowd erupted into cheers.

Dahlia shuddered, looking up.

Bazeema seemed to be fading into a wall. There was no time to stop and try to make sense of things.

Just follow her, Dahlia ordered herself.

Then all turned to darkness around her as a door closed behind them with a dull thud.

CHAPTER 15

They stumbled down a narrow passageway barely wide enough for one person. The air was damp and smelled like the water by the docks after a few windless, hot summer days. Dahlia turned sideways, slightly, to keep her crutch from banging into the wall. She had to move slowly. Dario nearly bumped into her.

"Sorry, Dahlia," he said. "It's kind of hard to maneuver in here."

Even Dario, for once, was focused and serious. *Where are we?*

Dahlia thought she knew the castle fairly well—she knew about the dumbwaiter, after all— but they were heading down passages with very little light. The walls were rough and uneven, as if they had been carved into the stone instead of built. They could have been anywhere.

Dahlia heard someone—maybe Hal?—take a sharp step and then a stumble.

"Watch your step," Bazeema warned.

Safi sneezed.

"I'm allergic to mold," he said sorrowfully.

"Come on, just a little farther!" said Bazeema, leading them around a corner to what looked like a dead end. But this dead end was wooden, not stone. Bazeema pressed up against it to reveal a secret passageway!

The passage led them to another series of cramped tunnels crisscrossing in different directions between the stone walls.

"So *this* is how you sneak around, Bazeema!" accused Gabo.

They had ascended a long stone staircase and come to a halt. Dahlia shifted her weight, trying to find a comfortable position. Another door opened, and one by one, they passed through the entrance.

"Gotta love secret rooms!" said Hal.

They were in a room that had once been used as a type of bathing space. Dahlia could tell from the large empty pool and the intricate tiles that covered the floors and walls. At some point the chamber had been turned into a storage room and then forgotten, judging from the barrels and pots left lying around. Starlight filtered in through narrow windows, but no one would be able to see in. Bazeema had decorated the room with pillows and baskets. It was downright cozy.

This is where Bazeema must do her weaving, thought Dahlia.

"This is my quiet place," Bazeema explained.

For some reason, Dario picked up a stick and began tapping on several empty pots for a quick drum solo. He was enjoying the rhythm he had created until he realized that Bazeema was looking at him. They needed to focus.

"Right. Sorry," said Dario sheepishly.

Safi took a sharp inhale and then stopped, fighting a sneeze.

"Dust doesn't bother you?" He couldn't hold back any longer. "ACHOO!"

"I like dust," Bazeema replied. "We're safe here."

Dahlia silently agreed. Dust meant that no one else knew about Bazeema's secret room.

"We're not safe anywhere!" snapped Gabo. "We're fugitives, thanks to Asha!"

Under his anger, Dahlia heard another emotion from Gabo: fear, maybe even sadness.

Dahlia tried to explain.

"She said she just wanted her family to have their wishes back."

"And you believed her?" he demanded.

Gabo was incredulous. He began pacing back and forth.

Dahlia flushed. She was about to speak again, to defend her best friend, when a figure in a cloak stepped into the room with them.

"It's the truth, Gabo."

Dahlia knew that voice.

Asha!

Asha pulled the hood of her cloak down to reveal her face. Star and Valentino were close by. Dahlia's first instinct was to hug her friend, but Safi, Gabo, Bazeema, and Hal all ran behind Dahlia. They no longer trusted Asha.

"AGGHHHH!" cried Safi.

"Hide!" ordered Bazeema.

"We're all gonna die!" wailed Gabo.

"Am I nervous smiling? I am, aren't I?" fretted Hal.

Bazeema nodded while keeping her eyes on Asha.

They weren't even saying Asha's name. It was like she had become a stranger, the enemy. Dahlia could feel them quivering with fear, with doubt.

Dario was the only one unfazed. He had somehow managed to get himself into a gigantic basket that came up to his chest.

"Oh, hey, Asha," said Dario casually. "We were just talking about you."

"Hey, Dario." Asha smiled sadly, but she had locked eyes with Dahlia.

Dahlia couldn't take the tension anymore; she had to know what was going on. Asha was her best friend. She took a step toward her.

"Please say you didn't destroy those people's wishes," said Dahlia.

"Of course I didn't," Asha replied firmly. "It was Magnifico."

Just a few days earlier, Dahlia had associated that name with great things. Now hearing any mention of the king filled her with uncertainty, perhaps even dread.

"Likely story," scoffed Gabo, folding his arms in front of him.

"The king was acting . . ." started Safi. He was going to sneeze again. "Awfully . . . awfully . . ."

Bazeema quickly pressed a handkerchief to Safi's nose and finished his sentence for him. "Awful."

"Simon looked like he was in pain," Dahlia added as further evidence against the king.

"Right before he squealed on us." Gabo frowned.

Safi cut the pained silence that followed with a loud sneeze.

"Are we just doomed now?" he asked, wiping his nose.

"Not if we fight," said Asha.

"Ha!" barked Dario.

He thought Asha was joking until he realized she wasn't laughing.

"Oh, you're being serious."

Dahlia looked at Asha, reading her expression. They had been friends for so long, Dahlia knew the difference between a slightly raised eyebrow and one that curved into a full arch; the difference between lips pursed into a smile and a smile that lit up Asha's face from within. When Dahlia looked at Asha, she was surprised by what she saw. She did not see defeat, or worry.

She saw determination.

Star and Valentino went to the windows, closing the shutters.

"What is she doing?" the others murmured to one another. As the room fell into darkness, Asha opened her heart and shared her truth . . . and her courage.

CHAPTER 16

Asha explained that the king had deceived them all. He was not the kind and benevolent sorcerer that he had charmed the people of Rosas into believing he was. He was far crueler than they could have ever imagined—leading them to believe that he would one day grant all of their wishes when that couldn't have been further from the truth: he was holding their deepest desires captive as a means of control.

As she spoke, Asha approached Gabo, Bazeema, and Dario, but they moved away from her. She turned to Safi and Hal, but they pulled away, too. Only Dahlia was really listening, trying to keep an open mind.

Asha clarified that none of what was happening was what she had hoped or planned when she wished on the night sky and Star came down after hearing her call. But she didn't have any regrets, because she now understood what the king was doing and why she needed to free the wishes of Rosas.

Together, Star and Asha used the colorful lanterns and objects they found around the room to play with the light and create different shadows. They formed a shadow of Magnifico. But his handsome face was twisted with greed and cruelty.

Asha told them how Magnifico was lying to try to cover his tracks, saying that it was Asha who was stealing and destroying wishes to distract from his own nefarious deeds. She had seen him destroy her own mother's wish with his bare hands.

The friends looked to one another apprehensively as Asha and Star used light and shadows to show more depictions of who Magnifico had truly become—looming over their kingdom, controlling the townspeople and forcing them to do his bidding as he held their wishes for himself or destroyed them to incite fear and obedience.

Asha was resolute. If they didn't act, who would? And if they didn't act *quickly*, then what would happen? The king had the upper hand, and he knew it. And there didn't seem to be any limit to what he would do to stay in control. With everything she had learned, Asha refused to stand idly by. She urged her friends to fight back against the king—for their home of Rosas, for their wishes, and for their future.

The idea of the future was almost frightening; they had been so used to the easy cheerfulness of Rosas, the promise of wishes come true bestowed by their handsome king. Now that vision had been stripped away. Yet, Dahlia realized, living under a false promise of a forgotten wish was not better than the truth, which was the fact that they were being ruled by a dangerous man.

Asha was right; there was no choice but to fight.

Dahlia understood. They couldn't stay hidden up in Bazeema's tower forever, and they couldn't submit to the man their king had become. Because it wasn't just a misunderstanding, as Dahlia had hoped. There could be no more waiting, and no more wanting. They had to go after what they wished for.

But the others looked at Asha skeptically.

Fight the king?

With what?

How?

With a grave look, now convinced of the truth, Dahlia stepped forward and implored the rest of her friends to see the truth with her. She knew they felt the same way she did deep down. She knew she wasn't alone. But each of them had to decide to stand and fight for what they believed in, too.

Dario jumped up and began pounding his feet in a rhythm.

This is how armies begin . . . Dahlia thought. *By marching together.*

Hal struck a bold pose and declared that the king had no idea what was coming. She was in, too.

To everyone's surprise, Gabo joined in next. He leapt on top of a barrel and let out a bellow that could shake trees as he spoke of their budding revolution.

Then Safi jumped in. He wasn't sure if they'd actually defeat the king, he said, but with all of them united in hope and determination, they wouldn't back down or retreat. Their voices, their feet, their spirits, were all becoming one. They marched in a line, together, encouraging one other. To run toward the problem, not away.

Valentino kicked over several barrels, and

some of the friends began using them as drums. Pounding together, the percussion of hands and fists echoed off the tiled walls. Streaks of light from different-colored fabrics draped near the lanterns around the room reflected over them and cast shadows that looked like their beloved kingdom, which they had created from different objects found around the room. The space began to explode with color and light, sound and emotion. They were going to fight together, for one another, to their last breath. To restore Rosas and take back what didn't belong to the king. They were united in their desire to guide their own destinies. To fail and succeed on their own terms. That was what they were fighting for, even if it was just them and no one else.

Except . . .

The door to the hideout opened and the teens froze.

CHAPTER 17

Had they been found out? Was their battle over before it had even begun?

It was Queen Amaya.

For a moment, Dahlia felt a pang of fear. Maybe the queen was there to capture them, to drag them back to the king.

But then Dahlia remembered the sympathetic queen holding hands with the heartbroken people on stage whose wishes had been destroyed by the king. She was with them. She had turned away from her own husband, the king. Or, maybe more accurately, he had turned on all of them, even his queen.

She joined their song.

She had seen the good inside of the king wither away. She had been deceived by her love. But she now knew the truth, and she knew he needed to be stopped. She was ready to join the fight.

All together, they gathered and placed their hands one on top of the other. This was their pact to defeat the king. There was no turning back. They knew too much to do anything else.

$$\cdot \cdot \mathbf{+} \cdot \mathbf{+} \cdot$$

For a moment, everyone stopped speaking, breathless from the effort of finding their own strength, their own dreams, their collective will not to give up.

Star glided over to the queen, inspecting her face curiously. Queen Amaya stared back at Star, equally fascinated.

"Hi," said the queen, amused. "Goodness!"

"This is Star," said Asha, by way of introduction.

Does Star know who the queen is? Dahlia wondered.

Before she could share this thought, Star made a tiny crown out of yarn and placed it on its own head, then looked at the queen for approval.

"Imitation really is the greatest form of flattery!" Valentino explained from where he had climbed to the top of a high windowsill. "Take it from me!"

"You are extraordinary," said the queen to Star.

Apparently the admiration ran in both directions, because Star blushed and waved away the compliment.

Then the queen's face transformed into a look of concern as she turned to Asha.

"You need to know Magnifico's powers have only grown, in the most dangerous way," Queen Amaya warned. "He is intent on capturing Star."

She turned to face Star again.

"He wants to take all your energy for himself."

Star and Asha exchanged worried looks.

Dahlia recalled the king's words as they'd gone into hiding.

But most importantly, find me that star so I may have the power to grant all your wishes.

"Then Star needs to leave, like right now," Gabo interrupted.

Star grabbed Gabo's head, turning it this way and that, forcing Gabo to shake his head no.

"Star won't go until those wishes are free," explained Asha.

Star stared hard into Gabo's eyes and nodded as Asha reached out for Star and gently drew it into a protective embrace.

"I'll make sure Magnifico doesn't get anywhere near you," Asha promised.

"Does that mean you have a plan?" asked Hal with an anxious smile.

That was what everyone else seemed to be thinking, too. Asha looked at all of them, hesitating.

"I knew it," announced Gabo. "She doesn't have a plan. We're doomed."

Suddenly, out of nowhere, Valentino fell from where he had been climbing and dropped into Asha's arms. She didn't even blink; she just held Gabo's gaze.

"Of course I have a plan," Asha said decisively.

CHAPTER 18

The first part of their plan was to have Queen Amaya get Magnifico to leave the castle by saying that Asha and Star had been seen out in the kingdom. The queen had looked for Magnifico before reporting her discovery to the teens. He'd been in his lair.

"A lair?" asked Dahlia, surprised.

The queen explained that the king had a chamber hidden beneath his study that could be reached by a concealed spiral stairway that opened up from the floor.

More secrets in the castle! thought Dahlia.

But the biggest secret of all, of course, was Magnifico's plan to capture Star. They could not fail in their mission; if they failed, all the wishes of Rosas would be destroyed.

Queen Amaya told the teens and Valentino to hide in the dumbwaiter. They were all there except Asha, who had left with Star as part of the plan. If Dahlia had thought the dumbwaiter seemed cramped with just Asha and Valentino, it was ten times worse now. Still, no one made a peep. No one moved a muscle. Their lives depended on it.

"¡Mi rey!" They could just barely hear the queen's call; she must have followed the stairs down into his lair. "Asha and Star have been spotted in the forest."

"Is that so? How fortunate!" the king answered. His muffled voice echoed off the stone steps.

"Shall we gather the citizens so they can see you capture her?" suggested the queen.

This was another part of their plan. They needed to gather the townspeople so that they could receive their wishes once the teens had freed them from the king's observatory.

Amaya spoke so steadily, though, she sounded as though this was a common occurrence. Dahlia knew that she was on their side—and that they needed to keep the king believing that she was on *his* side in order for their plan to work—but it was strange to overhear, nonetheless.

"Oh, we've been gathering them a lot lately, don't you think?" Magnifico replied.

The teens turned to one another in a panic. The citizens of Rosas *had* to be nearby to have their wishes returned to them as quickly as possible.

"I . . . um . . ." Queen Amaya hesitated.

"I'm kidding! Sound the trumpets, Amaya," announced Magnifico. "I'll bring back the girl and the star!"

Dahlia heard footsteps hurrying up the stone

stairway; they got closer and then, thankfully, faded away. That had to be the king running out of the castle. Still, the teens did not move—they had to be 100 percent sure he was gone.

Finally, the door to the dumbwaiter slid open.

"Okay, we must work quickly," the queen whispered.

"AND QUIETLY!" bellowed Valentino.

He looked around, embarrassed.

"Sorry. Goats have poor volume control."

The queen directed the teens and Valentino to the wish chamber through another secret passageway—a mirrored surface along the wall of the king's study. Their job was to wait for Star to return and then free the wishes by opening the roof of the observatory with a pulley system. Star would lead the wishes back to their rightful owners. Meanwhile, the queen and Dahlia carried out the third part of the plan. They had to get to the book of forbidden magic and see if there was a way to break its hold over Magnifico. Dahlia had volunteered for this job, figuring that spells were similar to recipes.

A large black hole loomed in the middle of the study where a floor should have been. If Dahlia squinted, she could see a stone spiral staircase within that descended into the darkness. She could hear Valentino and the teens remarking upon the wishes in the observatory through the secret passageway.

"So . . . beautiful," Bazeema sighed.

"Untouched by any allergens," Safi added.

"I've never felt so wonderful," Hal exulted.

"I have nothing to say," Gabo grumped.

"Through the heart we understand the world."

What? Was that Dario? Dahlia wondered from where she stood, as she heard Hal say, "Dario, those might be the greatest words you've ever—"

"Oh, look, hot drinks," Dario interrupted.

Hot drinks? What is he talking about now?

"Dario, no!" Bazeema called. "Those are dangerous chemicals."

Oh dear, thought Dahlia. *But that's not my problem right now.*

She just had to hope that Star would arrive soon to help her friends.

Dahlia wished that she were taking in the majesty of the wishes with them instead of looking down into a dank, dark stairway. The queen held her arm out to Dahlia to start their descent.

CHAPTER 19

In the distance, Dahlia heard the sound of trumpets once more, calling the citizens of Rosas together. They didn't have much time. Dahlia thought of Asha and hoped she was safe as she led the king as far as possible from the castle and the wishes.

The stone steps down to the king's lair were curved and uneven, so Dahlia moved carefully, making sure she kept on steady ground. A stench filled her nostrils, smelling of rot and smoke and something else. . . .

"It smells like sulfur," Dahlia observed. "Or as though something has burned. Perhaps parchment?"

"You've always had a good nose," the queen remarked as she held Dahlia's right arm on their descent.

She seemed surprisingly calm.

"That's why I invited you to the castle kitchen at such a young age."

"That was you?!" Dahlia asked, surprised.

For a moment she forgot to be scared.

"I always thought . . ." She stopped, slightly embarrassed now by her former crush on Magnifico.

"I didn't realize it was you," she said, amending her sentence.

Of all the surprises the castle had held, maybe Queen Amaya was the most astonishing.

If the queen noticed Dahlia's awkwardness, she did not let on.

"Oh, yes," said the queen. "I heard so many people talking about how you helped your grandmother in the kitchen. They spoke of your attention to detail and willingness to take care with every step. I knew you'd make a wonderful addition to the kitchens one day, if it was something you'd enjoy, which I suspected it might be."

The queen winked at Dahlia.

"I wanted you to visit the kitchens as soon as possible," she continued. "I remember being a child and enjoying such experiences. Trying things when we are young is how we learn about ourselves and get a sense of what we enjoy, how we are gifted, and how we can use those gifts to love and help others as well."

Dahlia was speechless. She felt the same exact way.

"I'm only sorry that your grandmother wasn't able to join you that day," the queen added. "I can still recall those cinnamon-sugar cookies you made for a picnic that afternoon. I'm also sorry that she didn't get to see you become the castle baker."

With that, the queen gave Dahlia's arm a squeeze.

"It was the easiest decision I ever made," she said with a smile.

"You? The easiest decision *you* made?" Dahlia stammered.

"Oh yes, the king *does* like to take credit for things, doesn't he?" The queen swallowed. "I thought it was harmless at the time. I wish I had realized sooner. . . ."

Her voice trailed off as they continued down the steps.

"Thank you," said Dahlia, truly meaning it, and also wanting to distract the queen from painful remembrances, just as she suspected the queen had brought up this story to distract Dahlia from her fears.

"I have *loved* working in the kitchens," Dahlia

added. "I've learned so much and have been able to make so many amazing pastries and feed so many people I care about."

Dahlia wanted to say that she had plans to make more, to invent new recipes, but she stopped herself. Everything was so uncertain. Maybe she was just fooling herself, thinking that she might get to bake in the future.

"And so you may well again," said the queen, patting Dahlia's arm, her spirits seemingly lifted to their usual optimism.

They had reached the bottom of the stairs. The chamber was old, much older than the rest of the castle or the king's study above. Rough-hewn walls were barely lit, and skulls and vials of strange liquids were scattered across worktables. Dahlia grimaced.

The queen led her over to one specific book.

"I've read all the other spell books in his library," the queen explained.

"There are thousands," said Dahlia, astounded.

"A queen must be prepared," said Queen Amaya simply. "I understand how to bind simple spells, if needed, but not magic such as this."

Dahlia knew what she meant by *this*.

This was the book of forbidden magic, standing on an altar made of gnarled vines and twisty tree branches.

The queen pulled out a small vial.

"Obsidian oil for protection from the pages," she said, offering the vial to Dahlia. "Cover your hands with it before you touch the book."

Dahlia poured some of the oil into her palm and then rubbed it over her hands, making sure to cover every bit of skin. The queen did the same and then gingerly opened the book.

"Look for anything on how to break his staff, bind his magic, or at the very least break the hold this horrible magic has on him," the queen instructed.

Her voice was regal and calm, but they did not have much time.

Page after page, spell after spell, the book promised power, greed, and pain. Dahlia felt ill.

Who could have written such a book? she wondered.

"This reads like a recipe book for the foul and savage," Dahlia said, with a look of horror.

She wanted to take a break. Each spell seemed worse than the last. But they still had not found what they were looking for: an answer.

The queen stepped away from the altar and began pacing back and forth, listing what they had learned—none of which was good.

"He's become practically untouchable. No metal can break his staff. No spell can bind his magic."

She returned to the altar and flipped to another page in the book.

Dahlia forced herself to keep reading.

"No one can bring him back from this," concluded Dahlia. She read the words on the page: *Embrace that which is forbidden but once, and you surrender to it for eternity.*

The word *eternity* made her shiver. It was so final.

The queen's face crumpled slightly. Her last hope to save her husband was gone.

"I warned him." Her voice was laced with both regret and reproof, but also heartache.

"I'm sorry," said Dahlia, looking down at her hands. It felt so private to experience the queen's personal grief.

Dahlia didn't know what to say or do.

CHAPTER 20

Their only hope was that Asha had managed to keep the king away from the castle, while staying safe herself, so that the people could receive their wishes. For the moment, Dahlia and the queen would go to where the rest of the townsfolk were gathered. There, she hoped to find the rest of her friends and watch what she wished more than anything would be a joyous occasion.

Dahlia and Queen Amaya managed to escape from the king's lair and make their way through the castle to the courtyard. They arrived just in time to see her friends come running from the observatory. Their faces were filled with joy. They had freed the wishes! Even Gabo seemed pleased.

"I always say, never lose hope," said Gabo.

After the foulness of Magnifico's lair, the open air of the courtyard was a balm to Dahlia's senses. The night air was gentle and warm, scented by the breeze from the ocean. Everyone was looking to the sky, where Star twirled joyfully, surrounded by floating wishes. People reached upward the way a baby might reach up to a loved one, laughing as they recognized the wishes, waiting for Star to bring them down.

Suddenly, an electric green light shot out from the observatory, ensnaring Star and all the wishes.

"Star!" Dahlia called out, horrified.

"Oh no!" cried Bazeema.

Magnifico's voice cut through the air.

"Surprise."

Magnifico was not in the forest chasing after

Asha. He was there, at the castle, and he had captured Star! Dahlia watched helplessly as Star fought to get free. Star gathered all of its strength and rammed against the invisible barrier, to no avail. The green light was relentless. Star could not escape. The people in the courtyard, so happy just moments before, shrank in fear and confusion. Dahlia and her friends clung to one another.

What could they do now?

Queen Amaya stepped forward.

"Please, no."

From the opened roof of the observatory where the wishes had floated free, a platform rose, with Magnifico at the center. The platform was surrounded by spiked black mirrors, and they seemed to reflect only cruelty and terror—the king's gleeful face, the terrified people below. The king was holding the same staff he had held when he granted Simon his wish. The mirrored finial of the staff cast the light that captured Star and the wishes.

"Good evening, Rosas!" shouted Magnifico.

His voice was too far away, though, and the people were too frightened to respond with their usual enthusiasm.

"Let's try that again," grumbled the king. He waved his hand in the air. His voice now became magnified a thousand times.

"Good evening, Rosas!" the king boomed.

The crowd still did not respond, but Magnifico did not care. He began to twirl his staff, causing Star and the wishes to spin helplessly in the air.

"Wow, the stars are really out tonight!" joked the king.

Though only he thought the joke was funny.

"That was mean, I know. But what can I say?" the king asked with a wicked look. "I really, *really* don't like being betrayed!"

Within the whirl of confusion that Magnifico had caused, Star was trying to comfort the wishes. Dahlia saw Star try to gather the wishes and hold them to keep them safe.

Queen Amaya stepped protectively in front of the crowd.

"It is you who betrays your people!" she shouted in a steady voice.

Even in this horrible moment, Dahlia felt a surge of admiration for the queen. How brave she was. She could have hidden herself away, but instead, she stepped forward, risking the king's wrath, for them, for her people.

The queen's valor was lost on the king, though. He rolled his eyes.

"Nope. Nope. I've had enough of you!" said the king dismissively.

He pointed his staff toward the queen and flicked a blast of green magic in her direction. Queen Amaya stumbled backward, crying out in pain. The teens rushed over to catch her. Dahlia wrapped her arm around the queen, trying to shield her.

"No!" cried Dahlia.

This was all going so, so wrong, so quickly.

"Your Majesty," Hal pleaded.

"Your little trick didn't work, Amaya," snapped Magnifico.

Star seized upon Magnifico's distraction to take another charge at the green barrier. This time, all the wishes joined Star, pushing up against the electric boundary.

"I still got what I wanted," said Magnifico, gesturing toward Star.

Just then, Star managed to pop one of the wishes through the barrier. The joy of freedom was brief, though.

"Wait! What's this?" the king asked. "A rogue wish?"

He opened his hand and the wish shot into his palm; such was the power of his magic. With a single gesture, Magnifico crushed the wish in his fist and let the broken light absorb into his skin. Down in the crowd, a woman cried out in anguish. It was her wish that the king had just destroyed.

Her family surrounded her, holding her in their embrace.

Star recoiled at the violence and hung its head in remorse.

"You shouldn't have done that, little Star," said Magnifico in a singsong. "The wishes aren't yours to free. They are MINE!"

The king raised his voice at the wishes.

"That's right! Now BOW DOWN TO YOUR KING!"

He punctuated his sentence with a wave of his staff and then slammed it down on the platform. As he did, the wishes dropped like stones. The entire crowd called out in distress, feeling the same pain as their wishes.

Star looked at the fallen wishes in shock, though for a moment, it seemed like the king's barrier had fallen. Then a voice rang out.

"Star! Get away from there!"

It was Asha, riding a horse into the courtyard.

Asha dismounted, keeping her eyes firmly on Magnifico and Star.

Magnifico smiled wickedly at the sight of Asha. With his staff, he sent out a lasso of green light, recapturing Star. With his free hand, he sent another bolt of emerald light across the sky to capture Asha!

CHAPTER 21

"Asha!" cried Dahlia and her friends.

Now Magnifico had the two things he desired most, Asha and Star. He used his staff to pull Star closer until they were face to face. Tiny Star did not look away but instead stared defiantly at the wicked king.

"You really are spectacular," murmured the king. "But let me ask you something. Where were you when I was young? When *I* needed you. Why did it take *her* for us to meet?"

By *her*, of course the king meant Asha. He

yanked on the green rope of light, pulling Asha from the ground up to where he was standing at the center of the platform.

As he gathered more power, the king seemed to become electric with green light. Currents flowed from his staff and his hand. Star and Asha twisted in his grasp, unable to escape.

"Well, hello, Asha!" said the king sarcastically. "So glad you could join us. I hoped you might answer a very important question for us all."

The king's voice, once so beautiful to Dahlia, now sounded like the low growl of a lion before a kill.

Star and Asha looked to each other with desperation, but they were defenseless against Magnifico's forbidden magic.

"Tell me, how's the whole 'taking your wish into your own hands' thing working out for you?"

The green ropes of light grew tighter. Asha winced and squirmed.

She's in too much pain to speak, thought Dahlia.

"What's that?" said King Magnifico mockingly. "Sure, I'd be happy to answer for you!"

The king slammed his staff down on the platform, and Star was sucked into the finial!

"No!" screamed Asha.

As soon as Star was trapped in the mirrored tip of the staff, emerald light shot out in all directions. Magnifico angled all the other mirrors on the platform so they reflected him on every surface throughout Rosas.

Dahlia could see Asha clutching her heart, curled in grief, as Magnifico towered over her.

"It hurts, doesn't it?" said Magnifico. "It really, really hurts."

It was hard to believe that they'd once thought this man cared for them. From the shuddering of Asha's shoulders, Dahlia could tell that she was sobbing. Dahlia wanted to somehow be up there with her to comfort and protect her friend. But what could she do?

This was it. Asha, Star, the queen—they had

all been defeated by Magnifico's forbidden magic. Queen Amaya was clutching Dahlia and Hal, trying to find strength, to stay in the fight.

Magnifico stood up straight and pushed his chest out.

"But I feel great!" he gloated, practically glowing with his new power. "And that's all that matters."

"We have to help her," murmured Queen Amaya, still thinking of others in spite of her own pain.

Some of the teens started carrying the queen to the castle, but magical vines slithered in front of them, blocking their path. Vines had grown over all the exits and were starting to creep across the courtyard. They were trapped.

Meanwhile, the king used his staff to whack the fallen wishes like some sort of sport. Dahlia could hear the sound of them rolling and clacking into one another.

"That sound is so satisfying, isn't it?" said the

king approvingly as he hit another wish from the platform. "Got some good distance on that one."

"Stop, please," begged Asha. "What about your people? You promised to protect their wishes at all costs."

Asha's voice was faint, but Dahlia could hear her.

Remember when you told us that Asha *was the threat to the wishes?* thought Dahlia. *When you lied to us.*

"I did say that, didn't I?" said Magnifico.

For a moment, he almost seemed ashamed. He looked down at the wishes and then back to Asha and sighed.

"I should thank you, Asha," said the king. "If you hadn't challenged me, I would still think I needed everyone's trust and that the closest I could get to happiness was being near their wishes. I never would have realized that I could just take what I wanted for myself!"

The king cackled maniacally as he looked

down at the crowd. His reflection grew larger and even more hateful. "That's right. I don't need any of you anymore!"

Asha forced herself to her feet and rushed at the king, grabbing for the staff. The king raised his staff, enraged that Asha was still defying him. He blasted Asha with magic again, harder this time. Asha screamed in misery. Dahlia hated that she couldn't do something to stop him! Her friend was in pain, and she could only watch, which was another kind of torture in itself.

Dahlia heard another scream nearby.

"Asha, no!"

"Hurry!"

She knew those voices. Sabino and Sakina had arrived in the courtyard in time to see their beloved Asha writhing in agony.

"Oh no you don't!" ordered Magnifico.

Dahlia could see a single hand: Asha was reaching weakly upward to the night sky.

"There will be no more wishing on stars ever again!"

Magnifico swung his staff, and an inky cloud appeared over Rosas, blotting out the pinpoints of starlight in the sky.

"In fact, there will be no more hope, no more dreams, and no escape," he bellowed.

Coils of green light began to creep out from the castle, snaking into the courtyard and capturing the townspeople. A coil crept around Dahlia, Amaya, Hal, Bazeema . . . all the teens. Even Valentino. Everyone! Terrified cries filled the air.

"No chance to rise up. No one to tell any tales. No one to challenge me ever again!" announced the king.

Asha twisted her body to look down at the crowd. Her voice was getting fainter. "I'm so sorry . . ." she called.

"Awww, did you hear that, folks? She's *sorry*," said Magnifico with mock sympathy. "That's right. Because of her, you all have had to lose everything."

Not everything, thought Dahlia, pushing against the coils. *We have the truth.*

Asha was fighting to sit up, using every bit of strength she had.

"No, you're wrong!" she called. "You can rip our dreams from our hearts. Destroy them before our eyes. But you can't take from us what we are. . . ."

"You . . . are . . . nothing!" thundered Magnifico.

He blasted her again, sending her tumbling closer to the edge of the platform. Dahlia saw her curl up in pain. But then she looked down at the crowd and locked eyes with Dahlia.

She can see me, thought Dahlia. *I can feel it.*

What could Asha say in this moment? What would her last words to Dahlia be?

Dahlia strained to make out what Asha was saying.

"We . . . are . . . stars."

The king blasted Asha with magic again as

she reached toward Dahlia, summoning all her strength, and began to sing.

Dahlia wondered at first why, of everything Asha could have done in that moment, she would choose to sing.

But then she heard her friend's words.

Asha was asking the people to join her, to stand with her. To *wish* with her.

But why?

How?

Then Dahlia saw the faintest glow of Asha's heart. A tiny bit of light that did not belong to Magnifico. A tiny bit of starlight that was *in* Asha.

There is still light.

There is still goodness.

There is still hope.

Dahlia thought of the moment when people gave their wishes to the king, of the light that emerged from their bodies. *She* still had that light, that wish. Something that Magnifico had not taken. And that glow looked like stardust.

Like Star.

Suddenly, Dahlia understood. It was as though different pieces from a puzzle in her mind fell into place.

We are all made of stars.

Asha's voice rose and quivered. It was faint, but enough for people to hear if they stood still and listened. Magnifico raised his staff and sent a final blast of forbidden magic into Asha. Her body jerked and went still.

Magnifico shook his head at Asha's foolishness, at her hopeless last gesture.

"You really need to learn to give up," he said.

Asha's light had faded.

CHAPTER 22

The song continued, though.

Dahlia raised her voice, picking up where Asha had left off. This was her song, too. It was everyone's song. Dahlia offered a promise to the people around her. This was how they would overcome Magnifico. She looked down and saw her own heart begin to glow. Light existed inside all of them, and everyone's light was connected. When each person joined in the song, the light would grow stronger.

King Magnifico raised his staff and sent a bolt of green light straight toward Dahlia. The green light struck the glow in her chest but then bounced off, hitting an arch. The arch began to fall apart. The teens pulled Dahlia out of the way of the falling bricks.

Queen Amaya took in Dahlia's glow and understood. She joined in the song, too. They sang through their doubt and fear. To dare to wish.

Gabo joined in.

Then their other friends.

The people around them lifted their voices and added to the melody.

Together, they made a wish that did not belong to Magnifico. To have more than just a wish, but the power to make it come true.

One by one, the hearts of the people singing in the courtyard began to glow as their voices rose in unison.

With hope.

With love.

With determination.

The glow from the crowd grew brighter, first within each person singing, and then all around as the lights joined together.

Asha stirred, weakly. She could see their glow, but so could Magnifico. He sent a broad blast of green light at the crowd. The light reflected off their hearts and returned up toward the platform, striking Magnifico, sending him teetering backward.

Amid the chorus, Dahlia could make out Sabino's sweet, quavering voice, joined by Sakina's, which was strong, clear. They were all emboldened by love.

Magnifico tried to direct a bolt at the pair. But the light from their hearts, along with the others', was so strong that he was blinded. The magic missed completely and struck a wall. The crowd fled from the crumbling stones but did not stop singing.

The king's staff began to tremble in his hands.

"No . . . no! No! Stop!" cried Magnifico.

He slammed the staff against the platform. Beams of light shot out in all directions, causing more walls to shake and fall. The sound of bricks crashing down could not drown out the singing, though. They were singing for one another, promising to help one another make their own wishes come true.

The glowing lights from their hearts suddenly shot up toward the platform. A single powerful beam of light aimed right at the finial of the staff. That was the power they had, the power of working together, of taking care of one another.

Are we winning? wondered Dahlia. *When will we know when we've won?*

Magnifico was now in a ferocious tug-of-war with his own staff. The staff seemed to have a mind of its own, hopping and pivoting away from the king until it broke free entirely.

Meanwhile, Asha had regained her strength.

She crawled on her hands and knees and joined their song.

Around them, the green coils of light were shrinking away. As people were freed, they stepped over the rubble and held hands to continue singing together.

Asha rose to her feet. Her own light was shining brightly now. The coils of green light broke as Asha sang to the sky. To the stars.

Magnifico leapt toward the staff, which was floating out of reach, still trying to get hold of it. Meanwhile, the wishes he'd caused to fall onto the platform earlier began to rise. His chest began to heave. It was the energy of wishes Magnifico had taken for himself. The energy raced out of his body and began to transform back into the original wishes of each person who had loved and formed them.

"No!" screamed Magnifico. "Those are my wishes!"

But it was too late. The wishes flew off to join the others.

Just then, a clear light shot out from the staff, all the way to the sky. The cloud that Magnifico had conjured vanished, revealing all the stars once more. The night sky sparkled with a new brightness, like bits of moonlight catching on ocean waves.

The people's magic was not done yet, though. The light from their hearts as they sang created turbulence, an inversion of what had been and what was to be. Suddenly, Star zoomed out of the staff, and at the same moment, Magnifico was sucked *into* its finial!

Star was free!

And Magnifico was ensnared in his own trap.

The green magic was powerless. In what seemed like slow motion, the staff, held by no one, fell from the tower, shattering into pieces at the feet of everyone in the courtyard. A cheer went up from the crowd as Star flew among the wishes, sending them back to the people. Each beautiful, delicate orb found its home.

The friends celebrated, hugging one another.

"We did it!"

"We're free!"

"Magnifico's gone!"

Their voices rose and blended together.

This was not the plan we made, thought Dahlia. *But we found a way. Together.*

All around them, people were crying with joy as they reconnected with their wishes. The cold was replaced by the warmth of their togetherness and the countless discoveries of what so many had loved and lost.

"The wishes!"

"There's mine."

"I can't believe it!"

"It's been so long."

"So beautiful!"

"This feeling. Come home!"

Asha and Star emerged from the castle just as Sakina's wish rushed toward her heart.

"Oh, my beautiful wish," she said.

Then she turned to Asha.

"My baby!" cried Sakina happily.

"Asha," said Sabino tenderly.

Dahlia and the others enveloped them in a big group hug.

"I'm so happy," gushed Hal.

Dahlia did not want to let go; she wanted to hold on until she could believe this was all true, that everyone she loved was safe. But then she looked up just in time to see . . .

Simon.

Simon, who had betrayed them.

Simon stumbled into the courtyard, clearly exhausted. With each step, pieces of the king's armor fell away, turning to dust as they hit the ground. The stone-faced knight was gone. In its place was the friend they knew—or thought they had known—so well.

Simon.

He was barely able to meet their glances.

"Well, look who finally woke up!" said Valentino.

Simon approached Asha. He did not hesitate or mince words.

"Asha, I'm sorry," he told her. "I'm so sorry. I don't expect you to forgive me. I was just scared I'd have to live without, well, all of me. . . . And I wanted so badly to believe in him."

His voice had returned to the one Dahlia recognized.

Kind Simon.

Sweet Simon.

"So did I," said Queen Amaya, stepping forward with all her usual grace.

"We all did," said Asha reassuringly.

In those few words, it was clear that Asha had

forgiven Simon. Maybe because it could have been any one of them falling for the promise of a granted wish. The group opened and took Simon in.

Gabo leaned toward Simon.

"Never trust a handsome face. That's why I hang out with you all."

The gathering in the courtyard was turning into a celebration as the sun rose, transforming the gray dawn into a sky swathed with bright oranges and pinks. Someone began to play a lively tune on an instrument, and people were chatting and laughing, talking about their wishes.

Then a harsh voice cut through the festivities.

"Hello? Hello! This is your king!"

The crowd went silent as Queen Amaya investigated the source of the noise.

The staff had broken into pieces, but the mirrored finial was still intact, and Magnifico was trapped inside of it. Dahlia watched as the king spoke from within the mirror.

"Amaya! Thank goodness! Do you see what they have done to me?" asked the king.

"Well, you do love mirrors, so . . ." Queen Amaya replied.

Dahlia, Asha, and Valentino stepped up behind Amaya to see what she was seeing. The face of their king—small, angry, and fractured—was trapped, glowering at them.

"This is not funny. Get me out of here at once!" the king demanded.

"No," Queen Amaya replied calmly.

"What? Are you—wait," the king said hastily, clearly unaccustomed to being refused. "Hold on, hold on. I may have been a bit harsh earlier. But remember, serving me was your wish."

A bit harsh? thought Dahlia. *You blasted your own wife with forbidden magic!*

The queen remained composed.

"You would remember it that way," she mused. "My wish was and has always been to serve Rosas."

By then, all the citizens had gathered around

her. They were watching and waiting to see what would happen next.

The king gave up any pretense of patience or regret.

"After everything I've done for you, for Rosas, this is the thanks I—"

The queen did not allow Magnifico to finish his tirade. Instead, she stepped forward and picked up the finial.

"This is the thanks you deserve," the queen declared. She handed the mirror to a nearby guard. "Hang it on the wall . . . in the dungeon."

The crowd let out a huge whoop to celebrate, while Asha and Dahlia led them in a new cheer.

"Long live the queen!"

"Long live the queen!"

CHAPTER 23

So much of Rosas looked the same but felt completely different.

The center of the castle, where the kitchens still hummed and bustled, remained the same. To Dahlia, the kitchens were still the best place in Rosas. The fire in the hearth crackled, and the smells of sweet and savory foods perfumed the air. The sacks of flour and sugar; baskets of eggs; wooden drawers of cinnamon, vanilla beans, cloves, and allspice; and crocks of butter still waited to be transformed into cakes and cookies and other delights.

And yet, the kitchens were different, too.

Dahlia looked around the space, remembering when she had first entered it so many years before. She thought of how nervous she had been, making cinnamon-sugar cookies and trying to get her grandmother's recipe just right. This was where she and Asha and their other friends had made so many memories together, laughing, sharing secrets, and nibbling on something fresh and warm from the oven. This corner of the castle was where she and the others had first met Star and where she had shown Asha the dumbwaiter so her friend could try to get her family's wishes back.

This was also where the previous baker had handed her a worn piece of parchment with the recipe for King Magnifico cookies. She had been warned not to change a single thing about them, and she had not dared. Her responsibility was to follow the instructions to make the cookies as perfectly as she could, and she had, even though she had always thought the flavor could have been better. The problem turned out to be not the cookie, but the king.

Dahlia took out a clean piece of parchment and laid it on the counter. It was time for a new cookie to celebrate a new leader in Rosas. A bit of food to add to the festivities. Dahlia began to sketch a new cookie cutter, one for the queen. This would be her first act as baker for Queen Amaya, a baker who was going to pursue her wish on her own to become the best in the world, so this new cookie felt very important. Momentous, even.

Maybe *too* important, though. The harder Dahlia tried, the more lost she felt. The drawing didn't look right. No, that wasn't it. She had drawn the queen, her face and her crown, just fine. But it didn't *feel* right.

It didn't feel right to just replace the King Magnifico cookie with a Queen Amaya one. Part of the problem all along had been that they had worshipped the king, his good looks and his power to grant wishes, instead of thinking about his acts or his intentions. They hadn't asked questions. They hadn't tried to figure things out for themselves. Thinking of the king as perfect had made her blind to what he was actually doing until it was almost too late.

Dahlia put her head down on the counter, frustrated.

You know what's wrong, she told herself, *but can you figure out what you actually need to do?*

It was hard to think of a new recipe, especially one that needed to signify so much! Dahlia pounded her fist on the counter. Trying to become the world's best baker on her own terms wasn't going as she had hoped so far!

You can do this, Dahlia thought. *Just think about what you are trying to say. Don't worry about the end just yet.*

She took a deep breath and tried to clear her mind.

The more Dahlia thought about it, the more she realized that Queen Amaya wasn't really a new leader in Rosas. In many ways, she had been a true leader all along. Queen Amaya had been the one to first invite and then later hire Dahlia to work in the kitchens, recognizing her talents and wanting to give her a chance to grow. Queen Amaya had been the one to protect her people and comfort them when they were threatened. Queen Amaya had confronted the king when he was wrong and risked her own life in doing so.

Queen Amaya had led them, without demanding their admiration.

What had her grandmother said?

Bake with love.

That was what Queen Amaya did—except she led with love. And they had grown strongest when they had cared for *one another*, not just the king.

Ah! Now she was getting somewhere. Dahlia wrote faster. She was getting a clearer idea about what she wanted to make. A reminder to love, to wish, to take risks. She began to create sketches for a different kind of cookie. One that wasn't based on a person . . . not exactly, anyway.

✦

When the first batch was ready, she covered the tray with a tea towel and carried it outside to find her friends.

Dahlia overheard Queen Amaya introducing two townspeople to each other.

"You long to fly," she remarked to a woman still aglow with her newly returned wish.

"Peter here dreams of inventing a flying machine," the queen explained. "You two should talk."

Dahlia went on to find Asha, Star, and Sakina watching Sabino play his lute. The old man was full of joy as people laughed and danced along to his melody.

The teens were there, too. Dahlia set her tray on a nearby table and whipped off the towel to reveal . . .

Star cookies!

Dahlia's friends rushed to grab them. Hal grabbed one first, then Safi, who blocked Gabo. Safi started to sneeze, but Gabo turned him away from the cookies, remembering a moment that hadn't been so long ago but felt like an age.

"Oh no you don't!" scolded Gabo. "Not this time."

As Gabo picked his cookie, Safi sneezed into his sleeve.

Dahlia laughed quietly to herself. Then she saw Simon standing nearby, unsure whether he was allowed to have a cookie.

Dahlia handed him one.

"Let's move on," she said.

Simon smiled gratefully at her as he took the cookie.

"Not bad for one hundred years old," Asha said with a laugh as she watched Sabino play his lute.

Sakina put her arm around her daughter.

"You got your wish back," Asha said. "I can't wait to know what it is."

"My wish? It's already come true," Sakina explained. "To see my beautiful daughter shine."

Embarrassed, Asha made a funny face as her mother pulled her into a hug.

Just then, Star seemed to get an idea. The ball of light got an *aha!* look on its face and flew off, quickly returning with a broken stick.

"I know. I'm sorry I broke it," Asha told Star.

Why would Asha be sorry about a broken stick? wondered Dahlia.

Star waved its tiny arms, mending the severed piece of wood. The teens, Queen Amaya, Asha, Sakina, and Sabino looked on in wonder as Star added more stardust, and the stick became longer and more elegant. It sparkled beautifully.

Gabo asked the question they were all thinking.

"Is that a magic wand?"

Star held it out to Asha.

"Thank you, but no thank you." Asha shook her head. "I'm no good with magic. I mean, I put a dress on a tree."

She did?! Dahlia would have to hear that story later.

"I'll take it," said Gabo.

"Nope," Dahlia interjected, stopping him from grabbing the wand. "It's for Asha."

Star offered Asha the wand again.

"But what am I supposed to do with it?" she asked.

"Be our fairy godmother," Dario answered.

"No, I couldn't be that," Asha laughed.

Then she noticed that no one else was laughing. They were all smiling at her.

"I could?" Asha asked.

Star nodded.

"We believe in you, Asha," Dahlia added.

With her friends and family watching, Asha carefully took the wand from Star, who motioned for her to try some magic.

Asha awkwardly waved the wand. Stardust shot out of the end and hit one of Safi's chickens, Clara, who was sitting on his head. As everyone watched in astonishment, Clara swelled to an immense size and then laid a giant egg.

The egg, of course, landed on Gabo and cracked open.

"Sorry!" Asha winced.

"Clara!" exclaimed Safi, shocked.

"And you wonder why I'm grumpy," said Gabo, wiping the eggy mess off his head.

Asha turned to Star.

"We'll work on it together."

Dahlia had seen so many expressions on Star's small face—happiness, mischievousness, anger, and determination. But this was a new one. It was sadness. And maybe a little guilt? Why was Star sad?

Asha understood immediately.

"Oh no," said Asha. "Don't look at me like that. I know what that means."

Star gave a tiny nod. Asha looked away, her eyes filling with tears.

"You're going, aren't you?" Asha asked. "Back to the sky."

Star gently grasped Asha's face and tilted it so they could see each other, eye to eye. Then, slowly, Star nodded.

Valentino began to cry.

"I will miss you!" The goat bleated. "My voice is really high when I cry."

"How can I ever thank you?" Asha asked Star. "You came to me when I knew only fear and confusion. You taught me how to be a better person and how to believe in myself. You gave me the courage to fight for what's right and never give up, no matter how hard it can be to make a wish come true."

Asha wasn't alone. Star had changed them all for the best.

This is why I picked a star as the new cookie shape, thought Dahlia.

"I could never do what you do," Asha insisted, looking at Star.

"Asha, you already have," said Sakina.

"Because of you, I believe my wish actually has a chance," Sabino added.

"Because of you, Rosas has a chance," Queen Amaya chimed in.

"Because of you, I humiliated myself in front of *the entire kingdom,*" Dahlia joked.

Those questions she had asked to stall the king had been pretty terrible. But she had done it for Asha. And she'd do it again and countless times more for her friend.

"Not sorry," laughed Asha.

"Me either," said Dahlia.

"And I might actually believe one or two good things could maybe be possible in the world," Gabo added reluctantly.

"See?" said Dahlia. "You can do anything."

Star swept over to hug Asha's whole face.

"I'm not ready for you to go," Asha said. Her words were muffled.

Star pulled away to look at her.

"I know, I know," Asha went on. "All we need to do is look up, and you'll be there for us, always."

Star nodded.

Asha tried to put on a brave face.

"Right, okay, I'm ready. You can go."

Then she pulled Star back in for another hug.

"Nope. I'm not. No, I am. I am. I just wish . . . I wish there was something I could do for you."

Star moved away and smiled playfully at Asha, as if to say *there is*.

"There is something?" asked Asha. "I have something? I don't know. I can't think of . . ."

She reached into her pockets, feeling for

something, anything. She pulled out a tiny ball of yarn. A remnant of a ball that Star had played with earlier.

"There's not much left," Asha warned.

Star took the ball and hugged it, beaming with delight. Then Star leaned forward and booped Asha on the nose one last time.

"I love you, too," said Asha. "Okay. Now I'm ready."

Star began to fly backward into the sky, waving goodbye. The teens, Queen Amaya, and Valentino gathered around Asha and her family, watching Star rise higher and higher.

"Wait! I changed my mind!" Asha called up to Star. "I'm not ready."

Star flew back down and hugged her.

"You can stay just a little bit longer, can't you?" she asked. "I mean, you are a star. I'm guessing you've got some time, right?"

She has a point, thought Dahlia.

Star nodded.

"Oh, thank goodness!" Valentino wailed. "That was just too much for me. I am only three weeks old, after all."

Asha picked up Valentino, and Star quickly created a handkerchief from the ball of yarn and dabbed the little goat's tears.

"It's been quite the journey, hasn't it?" said Asha with a sigh.

"You have no idea," Valentino agreed.

All this from one wish, thought Dahlia as she looked around at the people of Rosas, celebrating together.

Where could each of their wishes take them?

She could hardly wait to find out.

ABOUT THE AUTHOR

Wendy Wan-Long Shang is a children's book author living near Washington, DC. These are questions she *wishes* someone would ask her:

If you could have Dahlia bake you one thing, what would it be?

I love scones! I did not have a scone until I went to college and a friend introduced me to these baked delights. I would love to see what new flavors Dahlia could come up with.

For the first half of the book, the people of Rosas say, "Forget without regret." Do you have a rhyming motto?

Mmmm . . . what rhymes with chocolate? This is pretty close: Put some chocolate in my pocket.

If you could spend one day with one of the people from Rosas, who would it be and why?

Oooh, that's a toughie.

[These are literally questions you are asking yourself.]

Fine. Probably Gabo. I have a soft spot for curmudgeons, probably because I believe that most curmudgeons are disappointed optimists. Maybe Sabino, though. I love talking to older generations and hearing how their lives were different from mine.

Have you ever had a wish come true?

A long time ago I wished that I could get a book published. And now this is my eleventh book!